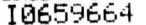

I0659664

Changeling Press. LLC

ChangelingPress.com

Ice/Cyclone Duet
A Bones MC Romance
Marteeka Karland

Ice/Cyclone Duet
A Bones MC Romance
Marteeka Karland

ISBN: 978-1-60521-950-9

Publisher:
Changeling Press LLC
315 N. Centre St.
Martinsburg, WV 25404
ChangelingPress.com

Printed in the U.S.A.

Editor: Jean Cooper
Cover Artist: Marteeka Karland

The individual stories in this anthology have been previously released in E-Book format.

Table of Contents

Ice (Bones MC 14)
A Bones MC Romance
Marteeka Karland

Ice -- The second to last thing I expected when Cain called Church was for him to resign as president of Bones. The last thing I expected was to be voted in as president myself. So when I found myself on a rescue mission for the daughter of the Devil himself? Well. I wasn't surprised at all. What did surprise me was the woman herself. Sure, I'd met her on more than one occasion, but the teenage girl I'd seen a couple of years before is definitely not the woman I pull out of the rushing water when she gets stranded in the middle of a hurricane.

Dawn -- Coming home during a hurricane isn't one of the smartest things I've ever done. Neither is getting mixed up with the man who was the reason for me taking such a risk. So when I'm stranded with water overtaking my car, I thought I'd finally tempted fate for the last time. Until my guardian angel plucks me from the water and saves me. In more ways than one. He's the new president of Bones MC and a man I can't deny I want with every fiber of my being.

Prologue

Ice (AKA Cliff)

"Got some changes comin'." Cain, president of Bones MC, wasn't one to mince words. I could tell by the look on his face whatever was getting ready to happen was huge. It made me nervous. Cain was also the only dad I'd ever known. He had always been straightforward about club business with me and my brother, Daniel, since we'd first gained our patched member status. The fact that I didn't have a preview of what was getting ready to happen made me doubly nervous. "I've given this a lot of thought. Torpedo and I are in agreement, so this is happening." There was silence around Church as we all waited for what I was certain would be a bombshell. "I'm stepping down as president of Bones."

"Fuck," I hissed.

My brother, Daniel, shook his head slightly, a denial when he knew Cain would never fuck around about something like this. "Son of a bitch. Why didn't he say anything?" Daniel's muttered question was meant for my ears alone.

"Beats the fuck outta me," I answered just as softly.

I'd have thought the rest of the club would be murmuring or protesting or… *something*, but the shocked silence around us told me no one else had had a preview of this either. I looked around at the faces of the men in the room. Most of them kept stony profiles, but a couple raised their eyebrows or shuffled their feet.

"I'm stepping down because I can't run both ExFil *and* Bones any more. Too old for this fuckin' shit." The officers smirked while the rest of us just glanced at each other. "ExFil has to keep going. It's the main way we fund Bones and keep us all comfortable without going too far outside the law. So I'm going to throw my focus into the company. Keepin' Argent Tech on our side as long as possible will help not only ExFil, but Bones as well."

"You sure about this, Cain? We still need you here." That came from Deke. He was closer to my age. A test pilot of the extreme variety. His grandfather had been a test pilot back in the glory days and Deke was more like him than modern-day pilots. He preferred to fly the fuckin' planes himself. Or helicopters. Or fucking hot air balloons. As far as I knew, there wasn't a thing the man couldn't pilot.

His sentiment was echoed around the room. Cain smiled. "Guys, I ain't leavin' Bones. Just steppin' down as president. I want to spend some time with my granddaughter and I'm not ready to hand over ExFil to anyone. Something has to give. Much as I love my club, I'm spread too thin. Besides, I can still be part of Bones without being president." He snorted. "And I'm fuckin' tired." That got more chuckles.

"I'll be stepping down too," Torpedo said. "Me and Bohannon are heading up another chapter in Nashville. Kiss of Death MC left a void there when they imploded that hasn't been filled. We're going in with the idea of stabilizing the region. Filling the gap and adding another club close to home to have Bones' back. We'll be sister clubs just like Salvation's Bane. To do that, we need to set up a presence there."

I glanced at my brother, who met my gaze and held it. As much as it was hard to live in Cain's shadow, I knew I still had a lot to learn from him. We both did. "Where he goes, we go." Daniel nodded his agreement. It eased something inside me. If Cain moved to South Carolina where the ExFil headquarters was, we'd go with him. It would mean we could help Mom with our younger siblings as well as keep an active role in ExFil.

"So. As to who's taking over." Cain glanced at Torpedo, who grinned and gave him a slight nod. "Obviously, the patched members will have to take a vote to decide, but we're going to leave you with our choice of replacements. I'd hope you'd give them our full weight when you consider them. Neither of us gives the recommendations lightly." There was a smattering of murmurs all around.

"This oughta be good," I muttered.

Daniel grunted.

"For Bohannon's position of Sergeant at Arms." Cain nodded to Bohannon, who took up the announcement.

"Stunner. He doesn't say much, but he sees everything." Bohannon grinned at the other man. "He's also harder on himself than anyone else could ever be so you'll never have to worry about security being an issue."

Someone called out from the back. "Just don't say anything about his wife." That got several laughs. Everyone knew not to mess with Suzie. Not that anyone would. Suzie was the pride and joy of the club. Stunner was her fierce protector and defender of her honor. The only man in the club who'd ever disparaged her had finally ended up kicked out. After he got the fucking shit beat out of him by Stunner. Twice. Pig had very nearly died after that last incident. Would have if Cain hadn't stopped it.

Stunner didn't say anything. His face was hard, the weight of what had just been put on his shoulders obvious and considerable. He wasn't the most sociable of men, but he would definitely have been my pick for SAA. Guy was protective of the club in general but Suzie in particular. And their baby girl? Yeah. God help any man who tried to date that girl when she grew up.

He was also Cain's son-in-law.

"As for president and vice president..." Cain looked at Torpedo. The other man nodded once, his lips curling on one end before speaking.

"We'd like Cliff to take on the role of president while Daniel picks up vice president."

"What the fuck?" My outraged question came out more of a husky squawk. This couldn't be happening.

Cain raised an eyebrow. "Problem?"

"Damned straight there's a problem," I said, my temper spiking even as I broke out in a sweat. "Surely to God there's someone more qualified here than me, Cain."

"Ditto," Daniel said, stepping up behind me. "For that matter, you've been running the club and ExFil for years. You never said anything about stepping down. What the fuck?"

"I'm saying it now. You sayin' you ain't up for this task?" He narrowed his eyes, taking us both in. I'd seen that look many times in the past. Usually when one or both of us tried to defy our father. And, yeah. We usually did it together, thinking we could get away with it. We never did.

"Cain..."

"No, Cliff. You guys are ready. Wouldn't have suggested it otherwise." He shrugged. "But it's not up to me now. You guys are our recommendations. Patched members get the final say."

"No need to drag our feet," Arkham spoke up. "I

vote we accept all three into the specified roles."

"I'll second that," Data said with a grin. "I watched all three of 'em grow up. Can't ask for no better."

"Well, that was fast." Torpedo grinned. "Guess we weren't the only ones who knew the youngsters were ready to take over."

"Anyone opposed?" No one said anything. I looked around the room, trying to get a feel for who would be my allies and who would pick at my heels, trying to trip me up. But I saw only friends. Family. Bones could be a rough MC, but we were all brothers. If anyone in the club threw their weight behind us, they meant it.

"Fuck me," I muttered.

"And ditto again." Daniel just shook his head.

"Well, we can't have a president and vice president with no road names." Carnage said thoughtfully. "You guys resisted until now. Got somethin' in mind?"

"Ice," Shadow said, stepping forward with a big grin. "I seen Cliff fight. There's ice in his veins when he gets focused. He's Ice."

"What about Dan?" I wasn't sure who spoke, but my heart beat fast. This was happening. I stuck my chin up. Well, if we had to take road names, I couldn't think of a better way to gain them than this.

Shadow grinned. "Cyclone. 'Cause he's a fuckin' whirlwind when he needs to be. Man can create devastation in the most stubborn of trailer parks."

"Oh, man…" Daniel sighed in resignation. "Really, Shadow?"

The big man shrugged. "They fit. You know they do."

"Trailer park. You had to bring the fuckin' trailer

park into it." Dan tried to scowl at Shadow, but the smile tugging at his lips finally won until he chuckled. "Son of a bitch."

I looked at my brother. The pride in his face was something I was pretty sure was mirrored on my own. As much of a surprise as this was, it made me proud to think the club I was raised in had handpicked for my brother and Suzie to make our home with, was confident enough in me to give me and Daniel the reins.

"They definitely fit." I held my father's gaze. "You sure this is what's best for Bones?"

"If it wasn't, I wouldn't have recommended it. You and Dan have lived and breathed this club since you first came here. You've done everything I've asked of you and you've learned willingly. It's time to put that knowledge to work."

"Then I'll accept."

"Ditto." Dan smirked as I looked at him in exasperation. "What? I can't say it any better."

Stunner just grunted.

"Well. Since that's settled --" Cain grinned. "-- Let's celebrate."

Chapter One

"Of course I had to come to Palm Beach during hurricane season. What a fuckin' shit show." I'd never admit it to a soul, but I fucking hated storms. The winds had just started to pick up on the hurricane forecast to hit the general area later tomorrow. Nothing heavy. Just a warning of what was coming. Fucking storm was a slow-moving monster. It didn't matter that I'd volunteered myself to assist Salvation's Bane with protecting the community outside of West Palm Beach. My only defense was it had seemed like a good idea at the fucking time.

The Bane clubhouse was up on a slightly higher elevation than most places in the outskirts of Palm Beach, but I had doubts the place would hold up. Thorn, on the other hand, was supremely confident in the integrity of his clubhouse. He was nearly as old as Cain but still held on to his club with a tight fist. Of course, he didn't have as many other responsibilities as Cain, so I got it. And really, I knew the bastard knew his compound. I just didn't like facing something I'd never weathered before. Call it a dislike of on-the-job training.

"We've withstood storms before, Ice. She may not look like much, but this place is rock solid."

"If you say so."

The other man grinned at me. "You ain't scared. Are you?"

"No, I'm not fuckin' scared! I just have no desire to be swept out to sea when anybody with any Goddamn sense evacuated yesterday!"

"We're stayin' here to help prevent looting. The

community outside of West Palm Beach needs to be protected and that's what we're gonna do." They'd sent the women and children out a week before. Most of them were in Kentucky at the Bones compound, along with the women and children of Black Reign. Being sister clubs had way more uses than what was on the surface. Black Reign might as well be a sister club, though no one wanted to have that bastard El Diablo hovering like a fucking mother hen. Everyone had a safe place to send their people during times like these while Bane and Reign provided our people with some sunshine and paradise during a long winter. Among other things. Not to mention, we always had each other's backs.

"I know," I snapped, irritated. "Ain't sayin' it ain't needed. Just ain't sayin' this is my favorite thing to do. I ain't a fuckin' storm chaser."

Shadow clapped my shoulder. He'd come because his wife Millie's sister, Venus, refused to come to Kentucky with the other women. Venus was currently the only female patched member of Salvation's Bane. Millie wasn't staying at home when her sister was in the middle of a hurricane, so Shadow had come with the little warrior. If the big man was nervous, I couldn't tell it.

"It'll be fun. You'll see."

"Right. Looking fuckin' forward to it." I was pretty sure the sarcasm was lost on Shadow.

"That's the spirit." Shadow clapped me on the shoulder with a big ol' shit-eating grin.

Yep. Shadow didn't get it at all.

Their intel guy, Ripper, had all kinds of weather shit pulled up on about fifty different monitors in his office. Only a slight exaggeration. Everyone still in the compound was in Ripper's command center, chatting lightly. There was tension in the room but nothing overt. They might act like they were flippant about the hurricane, but they were anything but.

"Still got several hours before the rain starts. Once it does, the heavy winds won't be far behind." Ripper had headphones on as he adjusted several things on more than one of the screens he studied. "Gonna be a doozie, this storm. Best models predict it stalling just off the west coast. That happens, we could be in for some historic flooding."

"We gonna be safe here?" Thorn's voice was soft as he stood behind Ripper, looking at the bank of monitors. I had no idea if he knew what he was looking at or not, but I'd bet my life he did. Which was why he asked for Ripper's opinion. Thorn wasn't a novice. He'd know the land around him and what it was capable of. He'd also know how to read forecast models of weather in the area. Why? Because this was his home. Thorn would know everything he needed to know about anything that could threaten his home and family. That included fucking hurricanes.

Ripper was silent for a moment, shaking his head slightly as if he were arguing with himself. "Not sure. If the storm stalls like they think it will, we might have problems around the city, but we should be good." He stood and pointed to a screen, circling a spot on the map with his finger. "That's us. We're at about forty feet above sea level while most of Palm Springs is around ten feet. If the storm stalls, they're predicting storm surge of twelve to fifteen feet above high tide. That will put a significant portion of real estate underwater. We'll be completely isolated."

"Not worried about that so much. But I don't want to put us at risk if there's no hope we're gonna stay outta the water."

Ripper shrugged. "Nothin's a hundred percent, but I don't see us being completely under water. At least, not the clubhouse. Some of the houses on the lower parts of the property might flood but not so bad it wouldn't be survivable for anyone in them. Just fuckin' scary and uncomfortable."

"Good. How long before the choice to evacuate is taken from us?"

"Another couple of hours? Unless we left on bikes, we probably couldn't make it out now. Traffic's too backed up."

"All right then." Thorn stepped back. "We hunker down and wait for this to pass. Sandbags are in place around the compound and the clubhouse, but I'd like to do one more sweep. I'd rather not have flooding that's preventable."

We spent the next couple of hours inspecting and shoring up any weaknesses around the Salvation's Bane compound. Most everything was done so this was mostly a walk through. I felt like a commander taking one last review of his troops before a battle. Ensuring everyone was ready. That the equipment and weaponry was good. In a way, I suppose that's exactly what it was, only the enemy wasn't one we could defeat. We just had to hold on until it tired itself out.

We'd gone out in pairs. Venus had volunteered to go with me and I knew exactly what the woman was after. I had to cover my mouth to keep from smiling. I knew this was coming, only I expected it would come from Shadow. I should have known better. Shadow wouldn't have hesitated to bring something to me, but he was likely hoping to enjoy watching Venus tell me how it was going to be.

"Have you thought about patching women in Bones?" Venus was a tall, pink-haired beauty. She was built like an Amazon and was just as deadly. I was six-five and two hundred eighty pounds, but Venus wasn't intimidated by me in the least. As far as I could tell, she wasn't intimidated by anyone. Which is likely why no one ever called her out about her pink Harley.

Ever.

"Yep." I had. Daniel -- Cyclone -- and I had already decided we were bringing it to a vote after we got back. If anyone deserved to be patched members, it was Millie and Cheetah. Millie was as deadly as they came while Cheetah had been with the club for the better part of twenty years. She was a warrior in her own right, but she saw her role as public relations. There wasn't a kid in town who didn't come running when she pulled that old-ass Winnebago into a Fun Run or into the mall parking lot during a Somernites Cruise weekend. She wasn't officially a patched member, but Cain had always allowed her as much say as any other member.

"And?"

I grinned at her. "That's club business, Venus. Bones business. Not Salvation's Bane."

She frowned at me. "I know places in swamp where even gators would have trouble finding your body."

"I have no doubt you do. But if that happens, you'll never know what we've decided."

"Let Millie in or I'm going to convince her to come to Bane. She only stays because of Shadow. If I get Shadow to move, Millie will too."

I stopped and turned to the woman, giving her a hard stare even though it was hard not to smile at her bossiness. "You can threaten me all you want, Venus. I respect you and Millie as both women and warriors. But Bones is *my* club. You don't get to dictate how I run my club."

We stared at each other for a long moment. I won't lie. Those fucking freaky pink eyes of hers wigged me the fuck out. As did her razor-sharp pink nails. She wrapped up the look with pink leather and pink motorcycle boots. It should have looked ridiculous, but it was just... *fucking creepy as shit*.

"Point taken," she finally said, breaking off to continue moving through the compound to the next structure we were inspecting and making last minute fortifications. I knew this wouldn't be the last I'd hear about it, but, really, it was already a done deal. We'd only waited to implement the final changes until me and Cyclone had settled into our new roles. Should have been done ages ago, but Cheetah had never pushed, and Millie was still relatively new. She'd taken on the role of a prospect, but nothing had been made official. It was way past time.

The wind was picking up. Still nothing horrible but I knew it was a portent of what was to come. And something just felt... *off*. I blamed it on my overprotective instincts. Since I was a kid, I'd always seen it as my job to look out for my family. Dan and Suzie had been the only family I'd had until we came to Bones. I'd brought my brother and sister to the biggest, baddest place I could find in the hopes the club would kill our nightmare. Bones had.

Over the radio someone reported in. "All good on the West end of the compound."

We'd divided into three teams. Seemed it was time to sound off.

"South side's good too."

"East side has building needing one more load of sandbags." Venus gave her report. "Found weak spot at basement entrance to rec building. Probably would be OK but considering it is basement…"

"Yeah." Thorn's voice came over the radio. "Sending Red and Grease with a load of sandbags. Everyone else, meet us there. We'll knock this out, then head back inside."

Reinforcing the recreation building took another thirty minutes. Venus was right. It would probably have been fine, but she had a keen eye for detail. If she said she'd feel better about more sandbags, I'd never question her.

As we walked back to the main clubhouse -- which was a converted fire station -- I nudged Venus. "Why not think about patching over to Bones? You can be with your family and still be part of a club."

She gave me a side eye. "So you're going to let women patch in, eh?"

I shrugged. "Want to know? Put in a request to patch over." When she scowled, I grinned. She'd make a great addition to Bones. Thorn might try to kill me for poaching his members, but I was confident I could at least fend the other man off.

Venus pointed at me. "You walk thin ice, Ice." She grinned. "But I will think about it."

Once back inside the clubhouse, we situated ourselves in the common room just outside Ripper's office. The man hadn't moved from there except to take a piss for the last twenty-four hours. We sipped beer and joked with each other, passing the time as the wind picked up in small increments.

"Lookin' like the bitch is slowing down," Ripper murmured. "She's an hour behind schedule from the forecast models."

"More fuckin' rain." Thorn shook his head. "Need less rain. Not more."

"Deck stacked against us, prez?" Tobias raised an

eyebrow at Thorn. I shook my head. Definitely felt like a stacked deck to me.

"What deity did you piss off?" I grinned at Thorn. The president of Salvation's Bane flipped me off.

"Wasn't me. Probably that fucker El Diablo." Thorn snorted. "He pisses off everyone."

We all got a chuckle out of that. Lord knew, the president of Black Reign was a force to be reckoned with. He'd inserted himself and his club into our world pretty firmly. Hell, one of his daughters was married to one of our enforcers. Sword was constantly having to run the man off.

Even after all these years, he still baited Sword. Since Magenta had accepted El Diablo fully into her life, there wasn't any reason for El Diablo to suddenly turn up on our doorstep when there was a problem. Magenta talked to him daily and went to Florida several times a year with her and Sword's children to visit with their grandfather.

I'd discussed it with Cain on several occasions. While Cain still hated the man on principle, he agreed with me that El Diablo did it just to fuck with Sword. And Cain. I thought it might go deeper even than that, though. El Diablo saw all of us as his family. He'd never admit it to anyone other than his wife, Jezebel, but the man worried about our clubs and the people in it.

Thorn's phone buzzed. He glanced at the screen and frowned, turning the phone for me to see the name that flashed on the screen. "Speak of the fuckin' devil," he muttered as he stabbed the screen, answering the call.

"El Diablo. To what do we owe the pleasure?"

"Thorn!" A male voice came over the speaker

phone.

I sat up straighter and frowned, meeting Thorn's gaze. Something was wrong. El Diablo, the former assassin for the largest, most powerful crime syndicate in the world, sounded... fucking terrified. Then, the bastard uttered the most chilling words I'd ever heard spoken in my life.

"Thorn, I need your help."

Chapter Two

Dawn

I was in so much trouble. And I was starting to get scared as shit.

My father had told me to stay in Kentucky. I was supposed to go from Lexington -- where I went to school -- to Somerset to stay at the Bones compound. But after the last couple of days, I needed my family. Especially my mom. I knew if I could make it back to the compound, Dad would be pissed I'd disobeyed him, but he and Mom would hug me, forgive me, and keep me safe from the hurricane. And everything else. I just wanted to come home and never leave again. And I was Goddamned sure never going to date again.

Black Reign and everyone in it was the only family I'd ever known. My mom and dad had adopted me when I was four and I'd been safe, protected, and coddled ever since. I don't have much memory of what my life was like before, but I knew I never wanted my life to be any different than what it was now.

Which was why I'd felt a burning need to go back to Lake Worth and the Black Reign compound for the Thanksgiving break. Mom and Dad had stayed. Dad because the men of the club would protect the community as best as they could from looting, Mom because she refused to leave Dad. I understood how she felt. I didn't want to leave my home and family to fend for themselves. Going away to college had been hard enough. But staying away during a disaster? I couldn't do it.

Only now I was stuck a half hour outside of Palm Beach. Forty minutes from Lake Worth. The roads were closed to incoming traffic and I'd just run out of gas. As I stood outside my car, watching the darkening sky as the wind picked up, I tried like shit to prevent myself from calling my dad. I didn't want to explain my stupidity, but he had to know where I was. He'd worry. And I couldn't ride out a hurricane in my fucking car.

I jumped when my phone buzzed in my hand. Glancing down at the screen, I winced.

"Daddy?"

"Dawn, sweetheart. What are you doing?" As always when talking to me, my dad's voice was gentle even as he demanded to know what was going on.

"I'm sorry, Daddy." I nearly sobbed my response. "I'm so sorry. I just wanted to come home to you and Mom."

"Sweet girl, we miss you, but it's dangerous for you to be here right now. You're nearly an hour away and the storm's picking up. You need to turn around and go back." I could hear the urgency in his voice even as he spoke gently. I wasn't sure I'd ever heard my dad scared, but I might have pushed him too far this time. I knew little about his life before he came to Black Reign, but I knew my dad was one of the most feared men in the world. To think I was the one to make him show fear nearly did me in.

"Daddy, I can't." I pressed my wrist to my mouth to keep in a sob of fear. The sky was darkening, the wind picking up. I could smell rain coming from the sea. It wouldn't be long before I'd need more shelter than my car. And there was literally nowhere to go.

"Yes, you can. Turn around and leave. You might get caught in the edge of the storm, but you'll be driving away from it.

"I've been stuck in traffic for hours, Dad. I just… My car…" I took in a shuddering breath. "I'm out of gas."

There was silence and I could imagine my dad giving me a blank look like the whole thing didn't compute. Or trying to take deep, calming breaths so he didn't yell at me. When he spoke, it was with calm authority. He was gentle but firm. "Keep your phone on and charged, sweet girl. I'm sending help."

I did let out a sob then. "I'm so sorry, Daddy."

"Hush, now. You be brave and do what I tell you. Stay in your car until I tell you otherwise, or you feel like it's no longer safe. I'll get someone to you. If not before it starts raining, then before there's a need for you to leave your car. Can you do that for me?"

"Yes. I can do that."

"If you have to leave, you call or text me first. Your phone's GPS is how Shotgun is going to track you. Keep it on the charger as long as you can."

"I will."

"I love you, sweet girl. Your mother does too. Everything will be OK."

"You promise?" I sounded like a child. Felt like one. I was an adult in my second year of college. I should buck up and take care of myself, but here I was. Calling my daddy to get me out of trouble.

"I won't allow anything else, sweet girl."

I believed him. Until the rain started.

* * *

Ice

"What the fuck is she doing there?" Thorn's normally calm control just snapped. "Are you fuckin' kiddin' me?" He had his phone laying on the flat surface of the table while he braced himself with his hands on the table.

"She was supposed to go to Somerset with

everyone else but decided to come here to ride the storm out with me and Jezebel."

"Rain's startin'," Ripper said from the doorway to his office. He leaned on the doorframe. "Wind's gettin' stronger. If you're sendin' someone after her, you better do it now."

"We've got eight men here, including Ice from Bones," Thorn told El Diablo. "I'll figure something out."

"I'm having Shotgun hook up with Ripper so you can track her. She knows to keep her cell on and charging as long as possible." This wasn't the El Diablo I was used to dealing with. Or rather, the El Diablo my dad usually dealt with. Cain would be just as shocked as I was.

"So, she's out of gas forty minutes out of Palm Beach. She's a sitting duck." Thorn scrubbed his hands through his hair. "Ripper, how long before the storm gets too bad to navigate through?"

"Not long. It's steadily worsening out there and this storm is expected to hit land as a category four or better. You might have thirty minutes before the winds make it difficult to drive through. Anything beyond that depends on what happens during that time."

"That's not long enough," Thorn whispered. "Not nearly long enough."

There was a beeping sound from Ripper's office. He straightened and hurried inside. "Shotgun shared her phone's secure GPS. Looks like she had to get off I-95 as she got closer to Palm Beach and cut across 714. She's now on Highway 1 just south of Stuart." Ripper looked back over his shoulder. "She's right next to the coast. Once the storm surge hits, no way she can stay there."

"Fuck." Thorn shook his head once, then found

Beast's gaze with his. "Take the Bronco. It's got a stable center of gravity for when the wind picks up. Take food and water in case you have to wait the storm out somewhere."

Ripper turned back to face us from his desk. His chair was across from the open door to his office so he could keep everyone informed and still be in front of the bank of monitors over and on his desk.

"I can't stress enough the need for her to get to higher ground as quickly as she can."

Beast stood to go, but I stopped him. "Wait." I met Thorn's hard gaze with my own. "I'll go. You need your men here to protect the compound and anyone in the area who gets in a bind. That's why you all stayed. Right?"

"This is El Diablo's daughter, Ice," Beast said. "She might not be part of Bane, but Black Reign has helped us out more than once. Besides, we'd never leave a woman stranded alone in the middle of a storm."

"I know that," I said, not wanting to ruffle feathers. "I literally traveled the exact route she's on now less than twenty-four hours ago. The terrain is fresh in my mind. I'll go after her in your stead. Consider it proof Bones will continue our relationship with Black Reign while I'm president." I didn't want to insult Beast, but he was getting on in years. As was Thorn. While both men were in top physical condition, I was in my prime. "Give me the Bronco and let me go after her. I'm the best person for this."

Thorn studied me a while before answering. "You're sure?"

"Like you said. I don't leave women stranded alone in a storm. Someone is going after her, no matter what. You take care of your territory and let me handle the outside business. I'll bring back El Diablo's daughter and we'll all ride out the rest of the storm here."

"If you can't get back to the clubhouse, take shelter in a parking garage as far from the coast as you can get. Stay off the basement levels." Ripper tossed me a phone. And a radio. "Satellite phone. In case you lose cell service. Radio's satellite too. If you lose or break one, you've got the other."

Once it was decided I was doing this, the other members of the club rounded up a case of water, some clothes for the girl, and some MREs. I raised an eyebrow at Thorn, but the other man grinned unrepentantly.

"A few rations went missing from the last mission I went on for ExFil." He shrugged. "Sorry."

I snorted. "Stuff tastes like shit, but it's better'n nothin'." I reached out my hand to Thorn, who took it in a strong grip.

"Be careful, brother. I won't tell your old man you went out in a hurricane."

"Ain't worried 'bout my old man knowing. Cain'd be proud. My mother on the other hand…" We chuckled. "I'll keep in touch. Keep me updated with local weather reports. If we need to divert, I'll tell you. Don't lock me out."

"Leavin' the gate open. There's always someone who didn't get out in time. Occasionally they wander this direction and we take them in. Few of the older couples in the area prefer to stay here instead of going to one of the shelters. Said they feel safer with us than with a bunch of strangers." Thorn looked like he was proud of that. I didn't blame him. We all might skirt the edge of the law, but we all wanted the people in our territories safe.

"Good. Be careful out there. Keep your eyes open and be mindful of the water. Keep your radio on."

"Thank you, Ice." El Diablo was still on the phone. I was surprised I'd forgotten the other man was still listening. "Bring my daughter back safely."

"I'll protect her with my life, sir. You can count on it." With one last look at Thorn, I headed outside.

* * *

Dawn

I couldn't believe I was stuck in the middle of a hurricane, alone and scared. The wind was howling and the rain was pounding down so hard I couldn't see past the windshield of my stranded car.

The wind tore at the car, battering it harder with each passing second. Sometimes gusts actually shook the car where I sat. I'd never appreciated what it meant for wind to howl, but I got it now. It bent the tops of the limber palm trees as leaves thrashed about in the tops. If this was just the beginning of the storm, I really didn't want to be here when it struck in full fury.

I shivered. Not from cold but pure, unadulterated terror. I believed my dad when he said he'd get me home safely. I also knew that telling me he'd send someone to get me meant he didn't think he could get to me in time to save me. My dad never trusted anyone with my, my siblings, and my mother's safety unless it was impossible for him to get to us himself.

I jumped when my phone trilled. My dad. Thank God!

"Daddy?"

"Are you hanging in there, sweet girl?" My dad had called me sweet girl since he and Mom had first brought me home from the group home where I'd lived. It was comforting to hear his voice and it settled me. Not much but enough I thought I might fight off the panic attack I could feel looming.

"I'm trying. It's raining really hard and the wind's picking up."

"I know. I know. The edge of the storm has reached us. Esther says its momentum is slowing down so it will be longer than they first thought before the worst of the storm reaches us. We'll get you to safety before it gets too bad."

"Kinda feels like it's pretty bad already." I could feel a whimper trying to work its way up my throat, but I refused to give in and let it escape. I could be brave. For my father. El Diablo. He knew no fear. As his daughter, I tried to adopt his mannerisms, but it was really hard. Like now. I wasn't brave. I was a fucking mess.

"I know, sweet girl. Now, listen to me carefully. The new president of Bones is coming for you. You've met him before. His name's Cliff. His brothers gave him the name Ice because he's cool under pressure. He will get you to safety and protect you until I can bring you home. You stay with him. Trust him. Do as he says. Do you understand?"

"Yes. I understand."

"He'll be in a Bronco unless something changed since I last talked to him. I'm texting you his number. If you have to leave the vehicle, you let him know where you are so he can find you."

"I will."

"I'd stay on the phone with you, but I don't want to use any more of your battery than strictly necessary. Keep your phone plugged in as long as you can."

"OK. I will." I took a shuddering breath, my control slipping as I spoke with my father. Most people never saw the soft side of him, but I could hear the concern and fear in his voice. Nothing could bring El Diablo to his knees faster than knowing his family was in danger. If that danger came in the form of a person, I doubted anyone could protect them. Considering the threat to me was a storm? Well. The fact that he'd gone for help from one of the other clubs he associated with told anyone paying attention all they needed to know. Yet I knew without a doubt my father didn't care if someone found out he had a weakness. Not if it meant he got me back safely. He'd contain the damage later.

I ended the call and took a deep breath, trying to steady my racing heart. The rain was still pelting down, turning the world outside into a gray, blurry mess. My stomach twisted with anxiety as I wondered how long it would take for Ice to reach me. I was alone in the car, in the middle of a hurricane, with no idea what was going to happen next.

There was a noise different from the sound of the rain or the wind. It was a deep, rumbling sound, growing louder and louder. I peered out through the window, trying to see what it was, but all I could see was a wall of water rushing toward me.

I screamed and covered my head as the wave hit the car, shaking it violently. Instinctively, I gripped the steering wheel even though I knew I had no control over the disabled vehicle. The car was pushed along by the force of the water, skidding across the road and slamming into a tree.

I sat there for a moment, stunned and disorientated from the impact. Thanks to the wave that just battered me, the water was now up to the doors of the car and rushing in fast. I fumbled with the seatbelt, my hands shaking with fear as I tried to release it. A sob broke free as I realized I might not be able to get free. I could die here!

Finally, it clicked open and I scrambled out of the car, the water rushing around my legs in a sweeping torrent. I hadn't even seen the water until it was too late! Now I wasn't at all sure I could get myself to safety.

I had minimal protection from the rain and wind. Thankfully, I'd had the presence of mind -- when I realized the conditions I was stranded in -- to put my phone in a Ziplock bag to keep out the worst of the water. It probably wouldn't help if it submerged for longer than a few seconds, but it was better than nothing. I shouldn't have taken off the ugly waterproof case my dad had insisted I use in favor of my pretty case with the glitter bling.

I needed to get to higher ground, or at least farther inland. I stumbled through the water, my heart pounding in my chest and my breath sawing in and out of my lungs as I tried to fight the water and get myself to safety. The wind was strong, but only short gusts threatened to push me over. As long as I was careful and those gusts didn't grow into sustained winds, I could wade my way out of this.

The road I'd taken when I realized they'd closed the interstate was near the coast. I'd felt safer thinking I'd see trouble before it got to me. That hadn't turned out so well. Fortunately, I was able to wade through the churning water until I finally reached the edge.

As I hurried down the abandoned streets beyond the water, I looked around frantically for some sign of safety. Most places had been boarded up days ago in preparation for the storm. Even if I could manage to pry the boards loose with my bare hands, I'm not sure I'd feel right about invading someone's business to save my own skin. Well. There was no way I was getting them loose on my own.

The wind increased in strength in small increments and the rain continued to pummel the land around me. I was soaked to the skin and the stinging water blew into my face with a vicious strength. It was impossible to see more than a few feet in front of me and I held up my arms in front of my face, trying to shield myself. I was scared beyond belief. I had no idea how long I had been walking or how far I had gone or even which direction I was going. I was completely disoriented.

Stumbling forward, I tripped over debris as the wind buffeted me. I felt like I was going to collapse at any moment, but I knew I couldn't stop. I had to keep moving, to keep trying to find my way to safety.

As I rounded the corner, I found a doorway that hadn't been boarded up. It was a niche in the wall. Not a great shelter but it would give me some protection against the debris that had started flying around in the increasing wind.

I'd started to sit when someone grabbed my upper arm and kept me upright. "Dawn!" The man had to raise his voice over the wind though we weren't to the point where he had to yell. Yet. "We need to get back to my ride." I looked up at the man who held my arm in a firm but gentle grip. He was gruff and insistent, and I thought I recognized him.

"Cliff?"

"Yeah. They call me Ice now. I'm takin' you back to the Salvation's Bane clubhouse. Are you injured?"

I shook my head. "No. Just wet. I'm sorry I left the car."

"The storm surge is starting. With high tide coming, the water's gonna rise fast. You didn't have a choice." He took off his rain jacket and put it around me, helping me thread my arms through it before zipping it up and pulling the hood over my head. He tightened down the laces so the wind wouldn't immediately blow it off.

"We've got to go three blocks that way." He pointed in the direction he wanted to take me. "All you have to do is stay on your feet and keep your head down. Can you do that for me?" Looking up into his face, I nodded. "Good. Let's go."

Ice had a firm grip on my hand as he led the way. We moved quickly through the flooded streets, the water now up to our knees and rising fast. The wind was howling around us. Even though he'd tightened it almost uncomfortably, my hood didn't last two seconds once we were out of the relative shelter of the doorway. My hair whipped into my face, making it almost impossible to see where we were going. But Ice was a strong presence beside me, guiding me through the chaos with a steady hand and a sure sense of direction. Every so often, he would lean in close to my ear to be heard over the wind, giving me a few words of encouragement or advice.

"Keep your head down, Dawn! We're almost there!"

I nodded, gritting my teeth against the driving rain and pushing on through the water. My legs were aching with my effort and my clothes were soaked through, but I refused to give up. I trusted in Ice and his ability to get us both to safety because my dad trusted him. No one failed my dad. Not if they wanted to live.

Finally, after what felt like hours of trudging through the water, we reached a parking garage. Ice took me up one level to the second floor. It was low to the ground but up high enough to keep us out of the water. I hoped.

He led me to the Bronco I'd been expecting and opened the back. "I've got some dry clothes and food. Might be too big for you but you'll be warm and dry."

Exhausted, I slumped against the vehicle, breathing hard. Once we'd made it to the parking garage, the going had been much easier, but the wind still howled through the structure and I was spent.

Ice opened the back of the truck. The tailgate swung out and he urged me behind it. He stood on the other side and turned his back, effectively guarding the open side from prying eyes. Surprisingly, the place seemed deserted. I'd have thought there would be other people taking shelter, but the town was small. Maybe they got everyone evacuated or to an actual shelter before the storm started.

He turned his head to the side, not looking at me, but like he was trying to see if I was moving. I wasn't.

"You good?"

"I-I d-don't know."

Carefully, Ice turned farther until he saw I was still dressed, then he turned all the way and stepped closer to me. "You're safe, Dawn. I swear I'll keep you safe. I'll protect you with my life." Intense, dark eyes bore into my own. He was so tall and big, he loomed over me. I should have been intimidated but I wasn't.

It was in that moment I realized why my dad trusted Ice so much. He was capable, strong, and fiercely loyal. He was also my calm in the middle of this storm. Literally. I also knew that like Cain and El Diablo, Ice was every bit as capable and sure of himself as they were. As I looked up at him, I saw a flicker of something in his gaze that made my heart race.

"Thank you," I whispered, my voice hoarse from the wind and the rain.

Ice's hand found my chin, tilting my face up to his. "Trust me to see you through this. Yes?" I nodded. "Good. Get some dry clothes on. I've got your back."

As I looked up into his face, one strangled sob escaped me. I thought he might look disgruntled or annoyed. Instead, Ice's eyes got big and he rocked backward like he was going to step away from me. Then he shook his head and reached for me.

"Come here, honey."

Having Ice pull me into his arms was the very last thing I expected. He surrounded me with his big frame, those strong arms holding me tightly when I felt like I was going to fragment into a million pieces.

I wanted to break down. Wanted to let the fear wash through me so I could cleanse myself of it. Get it out of my system. But this was only the beginning. I knew the worst was yet to come, and that was assuming we could get out of this stupid parking garage and to the Salvation's Bane clubhouse.

"Take some deep breaths for me." His gruff voice was oddly soothing. His arms around me kept me grounded when I knew I was so in over my head -- literally -- there was no way I could fight this on my own. I could feel the heavy muscles of his chest where I had my cheek on his wet shirt. The water was hot from the heat of his skin and as he rubbed one hand gently up and down my back, the tension lessened inside me somewhat.

"I'm sorry."

"No need to be sorry. This is a pretty scary situation."

Strangely, I felt a laugh bubble up in my throat. "You can say that again."

He grunted, holding me a few seconds longer before pulling back. "You can do this, Dawn. Get some dry clothes on and I'll do the same. Then we'll check in with Thorn and Ripper. They're keeping an eye on the weather minute by minute."

"I think Shotgun is too."

"I'm sure he is. Likely, he and Ripper are in constant contact, conferring with each other and figuring out the best course of action for us. They'll get me the most accurate information they can, and I'll decide what we do next."

Again, I nodded. "OK." I took another breath. "OK. I can do this."

He nodded sharply at me. "Of course, you can. You're El Diablo's daughter." He raised his chin looking proud. Of me? Then he turned his back so I could have some privacy.

There were a pair of basketball shorts and a dark T-shirt, as well as some socks and a pair of shoes that were all slightly too big but were a thousand times better than anything I had on. A couple minutes later, I tapped him on the shoulder.

"OK. Your turn."

"Eat while I dress. I don't want to take too much time in case we miss a window to get out of here."

He tossed me an MRE -- Meal Ready to Eat -- before he tugged off his wet shirt and wrung it out.

Any hope I had of doing anything other than staring at the magnificent torso on display in front of me fled in an instant. My mouth went dry and I dropped the meal packet at his feet. Not that he seemed to notice. Even as he rummaged through his pack for a dry shirt, he didn't take his eyes off our surroundings, looking for a threat or any sign of danger.

When he glanced back at me, I knew my face went beet red because I felt the blood rise to my cheeks. He must have realized I was staring at him because he smirked.

"Much as I love that look on your face, I'm gonna need you to focus, honey. We still have to get out of here and the wind isn't slowing down."

"Oh, my God," I gasped out. "I'm so sorry."

Ice actually burst out laughing as he tugged the shirt on over his head. The cotton material stuck to his wet skin and, though he got one side of it down, the other side stuck to his abdomen so there was still a fair amount of skin exposed, along with several slabs of muscle.

He stuffed our wet clothes into another bag, then snagged a couple bottles of water and the MRE I'd dropped before gently moving me out of the way so he could shut the gate to the Bronco.

"You ready to get the hell outta here?" He gave me a cocky grin. If the situation were any different, I'd have smiled back at him. Hell, I'd have done more than that. I'd probably have made a fool of myself trying to seduce him.

"Yeah. You think we can make it?"

He shrugged. "Not sure. The wind's picked up, but not as much as I'd feared. Then again, I'm from Kentucky. Don't know a Goddamned thing about hurricanes. Twisters, on the other hand…"

"Well, if I'm ever in a situation where there could be a tornado, you'll be the first one I call."

"Come on. I'll contact Ripper and see what the next move is."

He walked me around to the passenger's side of the vehicle and opened the door, giving me a tight smile. "Make sure you fasten your seat belt. No matter what happens next, I feel pretty sure it'll be a bit of a bumpy ride."

Chapter Three

Ice

Trouble. I was in so much fucking trouble. As I shut the door and started the car, I wanted to pound my head against the steering wheel. The few times I'd been in the same room with Dawn, I remember her being a skinny teenager. Cute but definitely not my type. But sometime during the last eight months or so, Dawn had turned into the most stunningly beautiful woman I'd ever seen.

Even soaking wet and scared, she called to me on more levels than I cared to admit. She was out of her element, but she'd done exactly what I'd told her to do without complaint after I'd found her. I wasn't sure any other woman I knew would have followed me as willingly and easily as Dawn had. Also, I was pretty sure El Diablo pampered and spoiled his oldest daughter to within an inch of her life. Though she was proving to be pretty resilient in hard times, I knew it was only a matter of time before she broke. I just hoped I got us to safety before she did. The very last thing I wanted to do was bring a traumatized young woman back to El Diablo. He'd kill me and I wouldn't be able to protest much.

Dawn trembled in the seat next to me. Her gaze was focused on the area around us. I'd moved us to the interior so that, even though the wind was still fierce, we were buffered somewhat. Debris blew around the garage, banging into the truck. She whimpered, but her face was set into a hard mask.

"Do you think it's safe to go out in that?"

"That's why we're going to check in with Ripper. If the weather's getting too bad to move, we'll find a safer place to hole up than here."

Dawn stared out the window. Her hair was plastered to her face, but she didn't seem to care. She was tough, I'd give her that. But she was also scared. I could feel the fear radiating off her in waves, but she was doing her best to keep it together. The last thing she needed was for me to lose my shit too. It wasn't the situation that had me on edge so much as my cargo.

I contacted Ripper. Thankfully, cell phones were still working. I wasn't certain how long that would last. Having the sat phone and sat radio put my mind at ease. We wouldn't be completely cut off from everyone half an hour away from home.

"I got her." I held the phone to my ear.

"Thorn has everyone at the clubhouse scouting the roads for you guys. I'll know in another couple of minutes what the road conditions are like." Ripper didn't sound concerned at all. In fact, the fucker sounded cold as ice.

Just as he spoke, I heard someone in the background. "High tide's makin' the water worse. The storm surge is just starting, but it's already got the lower end of town flooded. There's no getting to West Palm Beach safely and that's the way you guys are headed."

"So we need to go farther inland."

"Weather reports are saying we've already hit fifteen feet of storm surge with more on the way. It's only going to get worse over the next day or so."

"How long they thinkin' this fucker's gonna last?" I didn't really want to stay in the garage, but I also didn't want to get us out in the open. I wasn't worried so much about me as I was about Dawn.

"It's movin' pretty damden slow," Ripper explained. "They're sayin' about thirty-six hours. Maybe not hardly that long, but it's just starting so a lot depends on how it behaves over land."

"Christ." I scrubbed my hand over my face. "Is there any point in leaving this parking garage? We're too close to the shoreline for my tastes, but I don't want to put us in a worse situation."

"There's a Comfort Suites a little ways inland between the sea and the Saint Lucie River. I'm sending the directions to your phone and securing a room. Two with a connecting door because that's all they have on the first floor." As Ripper spoke, I got a buzz from my phone. "Head there. Let me know when you get to your room or if you have any trouble."

"Will do." I ended the call before looking over at Dawn. "We're heading inland. Ripper is securing us a hotel room. We'll ride it out there."

"If you're sure." Her eyes were wide, her face pale, but Dawn only nodded at me. There was no protest. No questioning me. She seemed willing to do whatever I told her to, which pleased me more than I cared to admit.

"I think we'd be better off in an enclosed place. This garage would do in a pinch, but it's not as safe as I'd like."

"I'd rather be in a hotel too." Her voice shook.

I reached over and squeezed her hand. "Just hang on with me a little while longer. I'll get you to the hotel and we'll be much safer."

She nodded. "Agreed."

"Good." I gave her a smile before starting the Bronco and heading to the exit of the garage.

The wind was howling now. The rain was more intense than even thirty minutes earlier. I eased out of the garage to test the strength of the wind before committing to leaving our shelter. Once outside, the vehicle rocked with each hard gust of wind, but I was able to make a slow advance inland.

As we drove, the rain pounded against the windshield so hard I could barely see. The wind was brutal and getting worse. I knew it was going to be a long and difficult drive, but I was determined to get us to that hotel.

Dawn tried to be brave, but I could feel her fear rising. Her fingers were digging into the console between us, her breaths coming in short gasps. I wanted to comfort her, to tell her everything was going to be okay, but I needed to concentrate on the road ahead of us and the map I'd memorized that Ripper had pushed through to my phone.

I kept my eyes fixed on the road, trying to ignore the chaos that was swirling around us. At one point, a massive tree branch came crashing down in front of us, but I managed to swerve around it. Dawn sucked in a breath and closed her eyes, but she was silent, as though she thought I needed silence to concentrate.

Finally, after what felt like hours, we pulled into the hotel parking lot. I pulled under the canopy to let Dawn out. I handed her my duffle and her backpack.

"Wait in the lobby for me. I'll park the truck and be right back."

She nodded. "Be careful."

I gave her a reassuring smile and headed off to park the truck. The wind was relentless, pushing against me with a fierce determination that made me stumble more than once. Finally, my clothes wet once again, I made it back to the hotel and jogged inside.

I found Dawn sitting in a chair in the lobby, her hair matted to her face and her clothes soaked through.

"You okay?" I asked.

She nodded, but I could see the fear in her eyes. "It was so stupid to try to make it home. The whole reason Dad had me go to the Bones clubhouse was because he knew I'd never make it to Lake Worth before it was too late. We even talked about it." She sounded so lost. Like she thought she'd messed up so bad she'd made an enemy of everyone.

"Why did you change your mind?" I sat in a chair next to her. I'd already checked the app Ripper had me download. Our room was ready, and we had a virtual key on my phone.

Dawn shrugged. "I wanted to be with my parents. Everyone else was in Somerset, but I knew my dad would never leave the clubhouse, and Mom wouldn't leave Dad. I guess I just wanted to be brave. Like them."

I could see a sad, miserable young woman looking back at me when Dawn briefly met my gaze. That was something I wanted to get to the bottom of. Not because it was any of my business, but if El Diablo made her feel inadequate, I'd kick his ass on principle. The Devil or not.

"Come on," I said, reaching out for her hand. She slid her smaller one into mine immediately. Probably a reflex on her part. I gave her what I hoped was a reassuring smile before pulling her to her feet. "Let's get settled in our rooms, then we'll check in with the club and see if we can find something to eat. Sound good?"

"Yes. Thank you so much for coming after me, Ice. I'm in your debt."

"We're going to be safe here." I squeezed her hand reassuringly. "And you never owe me for keeping you safe. All we have to do is ride out the storm for a day or so. Then I'll get you back to your father and everything will be better."

She nodded her head slightly as she allowed me

to lead her down the hall. Once we got to our rooms, I unlocked the door and let Dawn go in ahead of me. Ripper had gotten us two rooms with a connecting door, just like he said. There was a king-size bed in each room, and we'd each have some privacy.

Like I was going to sleep.

"Why don't you take a shower?" I opened my duffle and pulled out another pair of shorts and a T-shirt for Dawn. Thankfully, the guys had thrown in two changes of clothing for each of us. We'd have something dry for tonight and we could hang our wet clothes in the bathroom for after the storm passed.

She nodded, taking the clothes I offered her and ducking inside the bathroom. I took a deep breath and let it out before taking my phone out and punching in Thorn's number. He answered on the first ring.

"You guys good?"

"Yeah. We're in the room Ripper secured for us. First floor, so I'll do my best to keep us here rather than relocate to one of the meeting rooms. Hopefully it won't get bad enough to need more than one room. Tell him thanks."

"Will do. She OK?"

"Scared. Beating herself up for trying to make it home instead of stopping in Somerset, but she's not hurt. I got to her just in time, though. A wave nearly swept her car away. She's probably a bit banged up, but she made it here on her own two feet without much difficulty."

"Good. Want me to pass that along to El Diablo?"

"Nah. I'll give him a call. He'll want to hear from me since I have his daughter in my care."

"See? You already know how to keep your allies happy." I could almost see the grin on Thorn's face.

"Ain't about keepin' anyone happy. It's about letting the assassin know his daughter is safe."

"Very good point there. Let us know if anything changes or if you need anything."

"We will. Hopefully we'll just sit here for a couple days being bored."

"That sounds like the perfect thing for you guys to do."

Chapter Four

Dawn

Once inside the bathroom, I shut the door and leaned back against it. Sliding down the door to the floor, I wrapped my arms around my knees and took several deep breaths before I let the tears come. It was the only way I could safely contain what wanted to be uncontrollable sobbing.

I think I'd been mostly OK until the water had tossed my car around. That had kind of been the defining moment in this misadventure. Then Ice had come. I'd met the man before but when we were both a lot younger. I had been a kid, not even in my teens. Ice -- Cliff -- and his brother, Daniel, had been larger than life. They'd both been nice to me, but then, most people were. After all, I was the Devil's daughter. But they'd been different. At least, it seemed to me like they were different. Like they… *saw me*. As a person. Not some kid they had to be nice to or her daddy'd kill them.

I wasn't sure how long I sat there trembling, but when the shaking subsided, I felt strung out. Exhausted. Stumbling to my feet, I leaned against the wall again. Time to get moving. Lord only knew how long we had before the power went out and with it the hot water. Hell, there was no guarantee the water would still be available.

I hurried through the shower, not wanting to take up too much more time so Ice could have a turn. I'd already taken up too much time trying to gather my courage.

As with the first set of clothes I'd changed into in the garage, these were quite a bit too big. The shorts had a drawstring, which I cinched as tight as I could get it, and I knotted the shirt at my waist. No underwear. I hung up my other clothes before opening the bathroom door and exiting into the first room of the suite.

"You good?" Ice moved to the doorway from the other room, leaning one hip against the frame with dry clothing bunched in one fist. He was sinfully sexy. Way out of my league.

His jeans were wet, clinging to every muscle in his thighs. He'd taken off his shirt, and there was no way I could prevent myself from staring.

I'd seen a lot of shirtless men in the years I'd been in the Black Reign compound. Sure, there were things that went on I was never a part of -- Lord knew the club parties could be legendary -- but I was a virgin and then some.

Even though we lived in the middle of it all, my dad sheltered me from everything he possibly could. Unlike some of the kids in Black Reign, I was the epitome of a good girl. I never wanted to be anything but a good girl. Why? Because if I got into trouble, my dad would never see my wrongdoing. No. It'd be someone else's fault, and then he'd kill them. OK, so not *really* kill them but I was certain it wouldn't be comfortable for anyone but me. Me, he'd coddle and give anything to make it all better.

So, yeah. Faced with the bounty of a man in front of me, there was no way I could keep from staring. If we holed up in this motel for more than a day, it was going to get supremely uncomfortable. Because there was no way I could keep from looking at Ice. He had my full, undivided attention.

"Um, yeah." I tried to eke out a smile when I was still reeling. Not only had I nearly died today, but now I was presented with the most delicious man I'd ever seen and had no idea what to do with him. I was sure

I'd reached the end of any endurance I had. "I'm fine."

He winced. "Honey, I'm not a ladies' man or anything, but I have a wonderful mother who taught me when a woman says she's fine, she's anything but." He stood and crossed the room toward me slowly. He had a concerned look on his face, but the whole situation reminded me of a panther stalking his prey. "Did you get hurt before or are you just on overload?"

"Overload," I managed to say. I looked down at my feet, not sure of what to do.

Ice tilted my chin up so that I was forced to look him in the eye. "What do you need, honey?" he asked softly, his eyes searching mine.

I felt my cheeks flush as his proximity made my heart race. "I don't know," I admitted, feeling vulnerable and exposed. "Everything's just been more than I'm used to handling." I tried to snort out a deprecating laugh but wasn't sure I was believable. "Believe it or not, my dad always made sure me and my mom were never in Florida when a hurricane was in the area. Took me several years before I realized what he was doing."

Ice grinned. "Yeah. I can see him doing that. Why don't you lie down for a bit? I've ordered room service. As long as the power stays on, they're going to keep cooking. They've assured me they have plenty of sandwich meat, fruit, and cheeses to last a few days if need be." He brushed a lock of wet hair off my cheek gently. "I'm gonna run through the shower real quick. I should be out before they get here, but if I'm not, tell them to set the tray outside the door. Don't let anyone inside and don't leave the room. Understand?"

"What? Why? We're not in danger from anything other than the storm. Right?"

"Of course not. Call it an abundance of caution."

He grinned at me. "I just like breathing. Having someone snag you under my nose while I'm in the shower is a good way to have your dad kill my sorry ass." I couldn't help the grin and giggle that escaped. "There," Ice said with a satisfied smile. "That's much better. I like that smile on your face rather than fear."

Then Ice did something I wasn't expecting. He leaned in and kissed my forehead before heading to the bathroom without a backward glance.

* * *

Ice

I'd only thought I was fucked before. Standing in the bathroom, my back to the closed door, I took in a deep breath, trying to cleanse myself of… her. Dawn.

There was a clean, fresh scent clinging to her. Like honeysuckle or jasmine. Her small frame was dwarfed by my own large body. When she looked up at me with hope and fear shining in her eyes, I knew she was putty in my hands. When that look turned hungry? Well. It'd take a stronger man than me to ignore the need she projected. If we were in any other situation and this was any other woman besides El Diablo's daughter, I'd gladly take what she offered when she stood staring at my bare chest.

But we were in a bad situation. And this was El Diablo's daughter. It wasn't that she wasn't worth the risk. Hell yeah, she was worth it! But I had too much respect for El Diablo, even if he was a thorn in my dad's side, and I'd never put my needs ahead of my club's. Not for sex. Even if she was the most desirable woman I'd ever seen.

With a grunt and a shake of my head, I stripped and ran through the shower. I didn't want to be in the bathroom when our food arrived. Not because I thought anyone would hurt Dawn but because it was my job to see to her safety and comfort.

As I soaped my body, I stared down at my hard cock. The asshole had a mind of its own. It wanted Dawn as much as I did, but it didn't understand why we couldn't have her.

I gripped my dick, stroking firmly to get a little relief. The last thing I needed to do was leave this room in gym shorts with my cock standing at full attention. Dawn would probably hide under the bed and I wouldn't blame her. She knew me but not that well. Definitely not well enough for me to be walking around her with my cock at full attention.

I covered my dick, wrapping my hand tight around the base. Closing my eyes for one second, I could see Dawn's face looking up at me, her lips parting to take my dick between her lips and suck. Would that be something she'd enjoy? Would she close her eyes in bliss as she hummed around me?

"Christ!"

I threw back my head and groaned as I came. My cock pulsed out an angry beat with every spurt. Not nearly enough.

"Fuck."

I rinsed quickly, adjusted the water temperature, and finished up my shower. Thankfully, the hotel furnished a couple of toothbrushes. I brushed my teeth and dressed before I opened the door.

Without even trying, I met Dawn's gaze where she sat on the edge of the bed.

Not for you, asshole. She's El Diablo's daughter! Not only would he kill me for lusting after his daughter, but it would put strain on our clubs' relationship. Which would negate any good I might be doing by rescuing her.

"You didn't want to lie down?" I tried to sound as gentle as I could be. The poor girl had to be close to her breaking point.

She shook her head but didn't look at me.

"You good, Dawn?" She nodded her head. "Yeah," I said, approaching her carefully. "You're not good at all, are you?"

Right before my eyes, Dawn lost her fight to stay in control. She started shaking, then she broke down in tears, sobbing uncontrollably.

"Fuck. Come here, honey." I pulled her up from the bed into my arms before sitting back on the bed with her. She curled up in my lap, clinging to me with a death grip. Though her tears were like daggers through my fucking chest, I loved that she was trusting me with this. That she was taking refuge in my arms. That she felt safe enough to let it out.

"It's okay. I've got you," I whispered, kissing the top of her head. "I've got you, Dawn. We're gonna make it through this together. I promise."

Not wanting to make anything harder for her to process, I kept stroking her hair and back to soothe her. I had no clue what she needed and I wasn't sure I was even doing the right thing. I was a stranger to her, and here I was in her personal space. But Goddamn if it didn't feel right!

"I'm sorry," Dawn mumbled into my chest, sniffing.

"There's nothing to be sorry for," I replied.

"I don't know what's wrong with me. I never act like this."

She was too upset to look at me, but she did bury herself farther into my chest, which filled me with more satisfaction than I ever thought possible.

There was a knock at the door. Room service.

"Great timing," I muttered but made no move to get up.

"Aren't you going to get that?" She looked up at me with big eyes. She made no move to get off me, and I just tightened my arms around her.

"It's just room service."

When the knock came again, she sighed, leaned in one last time and took a deep breath. Then she slid off my lap and sat in a nearby chair. I gave her a smile before crossing to the other room and opening the door. I tipped the guy and took the tray, placing it on the table.

"I went with a burger and fries. You good with that?"

"Yeah, but I'm not really hungry."

I hardened my voice. "You'll eat what you can. I don't know how long this will last and, while I'm confident we can ride the storm out here, I'd rather us be prepared if we need to leave. That means you need your strength."

"I know," she said softly. "You're right." Dawn stood and went to the small table to sit. "Thank you, by the way. For saving me out there."

"No need for thanks. I was glad to do it."

"Because of my father?"

I frowned. "Why would you say that?"

She shook her head. "No reason."

I studied her for a long moment. She didn't make a move to remove the lid from her food, so I did it for her. "I came after you for a few reasons." I removed the lid from my own plate and passed her the mustard and ketchup. "El Diablo called Thorn in… distress. He was frantic to get someone to you and knew he didn't have time to himself. Everyone but a small number from Salvation's Bane is in Kentucky with Bones."

"Where I was supposed to be." She looked down at her plate without interest. I thought I saw sadness and guilt on her face, but I didn't know her well enough to make that call.

"Thorn is very protective of his territory and the people in it. He was going to send Beast, but I talked him out of it."

She looked up at me, her lips parting. "Why would you do that?"

"Like I said. Several reasons. First, El Diablo dropped that on Thorn. President of Bane. If he couldn't go, he couldn't very well give it to someone other than his vice president or the president of another club he trusted. I volunteered because he needed to be with his club and the local community. They don't often reach out to them but in situations like this? Yeah. He probably had several people come for shelter once the winds started in force."

"That was nice of you." Her voice was soft and she wouldn't meet my gaze.

"By volunteering, I not only took a burden from Thorn, but let both him and El Diablo know that, as the new president of Bones, I intend to continue the supportive relationships we've forged over the years."

She glanced away. "Always my dad," she muttered.

I reached across the table and placed my hand over hers. "Dawn, what's going on? Why were you really so intent on getting back to Lake Worth?"

"It's nothing. Poor judgment." She tugged her hand from under mine and picked up a fry and nibbled, not really making an effort to eat.

"Uh-huh." I sat back and crossed my arms over my chest. "You know, we're gonna be here for several hours. Tell me what's going on."

She sighed and looked away, but I could tell she was considering it. "I have some things…" She trailed off. "Well, one thing."

"Money?"

"No." She sighed, looking down at her plate, her shoulders slumped. She picked up another fry and put it into her mouth and chewed. I thought it was more to give her a moment to gather her thoughts before she continued the conversation. "It's stupid."

"Honey, if it got you upset enough to run to your family in the middle of a storm, it's not stupid. Tell me."

"You promise not to tell Dad?"

"Nope. I ain't a dumb fuck. But I promise not to tell him if it doesn't endanger your safety."

Dawn nodded, then hung her head. "I can respect that. Everyone who really knows my dad is afraid of him."

"Honey, he's the world's most deadly assassin." I raised an eyebrow at her. "Anyone who knows your dad would be a fool not to be afraid of him."

"What about you?" The girl had the most beautiful sapphire eyes to go with straight, shoulder-length, blue-black hair. She was an exotic beauty but lacked the confidence she should have given her status in Black Reign as the president's daughter, not to mention just being El Diablo's daughter.

"I have a healthy caution when it comes to him. I've not given him any reason to come after me, but I'm not looking to intentionally provoke him either."

She sat back in her chair, not touching more of her food, then took a deep breath. "I got dumped."

That… didn't compute. "Dumped?"

"Yeah. The guy I was dating got tired of waiting on me. So one night he decided to get even."

Everything inside me stilled. I had no idea exactly what had happened, but I knew it wasn't good. There was no way I could get away with not telling El Diablo what she was about to say, and I might have to make a trip somewhere to kill a motherfucker.

"Define 'got tired of waiting' on you." I tried to keep my voice neutral, but when her head snapped up and she winced, I knew I hadn't been very successful.

"I wouldn't sleep with him." Her voice was a mere thread of sound. "I wasn't ready for that, and I knew from the moment I met him it wouldn't be him."

"He try to rape you?"

"No. But he wasn't happy I wouldn't have sex with him. That's when he broke up with me. Because he said if he was in a relationship with someone, he wanted sex to be involved. 'A man has needs' and all that shit."

"How'd he get even?"

"Stole my wallet. Drained my bank account. Maxed out my credit card. I had my bank account set to notify me of any transactions or it would have been a while before I realized. Normally I wouldn't have even checked my credit card account, but after I figured out what he'd done, I looked. I guess he used my credit card first, then went after my bank account."

"He have your PIN number?"

"Yeah. Watched me get money from an ATM, I guess. The bank said every transaction was made using my PIN. I'm surprised Dad hasn't said anything about it yet. He has to know."

"Did you call this asshole out?"

"No. I just got in my car and headed for home. I wanted to be with my family. Where I knew the rules and no one was out to fuck me over."

"Where's the bastard now?"

"Don't know. Don't care. It's going to disappoint my dad, but I'm not going back to school."

"Gonna need a name, sweetheart." Because I was definitely going to take that motherfucker down. I got the feeling she was holding back on me, but I'd take her at her word. For now.

She shook her head. "No. I tell you, you tell my dad. Then the guy disappears. I know my dad's a killer, but I don't want him killing on my behalf. Especially over something like this."

"Like what? The fact that he ripped you off? Or that he tried to pressure you into having sex with him?"

"Either. He didn't assault me."

"He try to shame you into fuckin' him? Make you feel like you owed him?" When her eyes went wide and her lips parted, I knew I'd hit the mark. "That's what I thought. You will tell me his name and anything else you know about him, and I'll deal with him."

"I can't do that," she whispered. "I know what happens if I do." Then she tilted her head. "Is this to get in good with my father? You said you wanted him to know Bones would be an ally with you as president."

I laughed, but it was a humorless sound. "Sweetheart, I don't need to get in good with your father. He already knows what I'm capable of. If he didn't, there's no way he'd have agreed to let me take this on instead of Thorn. Right now, I'm more concerned with making sure that asshole never comes near you again. He doesn't deserve you."

"I don't know about that, but he's done with me. And I'm done with him."

"Good. Now. Finish eating. I'm going to call El

Diablo and let him know you're safe."

She gasped. "Are you going to tell him about... uh..."

"No. Not unless he asks me outright. Not yet anyway. But I won't lie to him."

"Please, Ice." Her gaze was beseeching with tears threatening to overflow. I wasn't sure I could take more of her tears. They affected me like nothing else before. I wasn't a man who went around being mean to women, but tears didn't affect me unless they were my mother's or Suzie's. Or, apparently, Dawn's.

"I won't lie to him. I should tell him about this, but he's not a threat to your safety. Whether or not I have to kill him will depend entirely on what my club can find out about him. I won't take this to Thorn or El Diablo but will keep it in Bones. For now. But this conversation isn't over."

"I guess that's the best I should have expected."

"*Better* than you should have expected," I corrected. "I won't come between a father and his daughter unless he's hurting her."

She nodded and looked back down at her food. "I'm sorry."

"No need to be sorry. Why don't you lie down and rest when you're done eating? I'm going to bully someone into giving me another set of heavy drapes to go over the windows in your room. These buildings are built to withstand hurricanes, but I don't want to take a chance something breaks the window and hurts you."

Dawn nodded but didn't look back up at me. I shook my head, needing to comfort her, but it wasn't my place. Stepping out into the hall, I took out my cell and called El Diablo. Not surprisingly, the man answered on the first wring.

"Where's my daughter?" Yeah. That was the voice of the world's deadliest assassin.

"We're at a hotel. Ripper has the details because he secured the rooms."

"Rooms?"

"Well, yeah. It's an adjoining suite. Not that I plan on shutting the door. But she'll have her privacy. You wanted me in the same room with her?"

"Fuck no! Just didn't want her alone during the storm in case of problems."

"Understood. We're safe for now. She's dry, clean, and fed. I'm going to get extra protection for the windows now, then I'll be with her for the duration. I'll bring her home safe."

"Good." The other man took a deep breath. "That's good. I owe you a debt, Ice. I won't forget."

"Consider this a gesture of good faith. I can't promise we'll be more friendly than when Cain was president, but I can promise we'll still be allies."

El Diablo hesitated for a moment before responding, "Good." The man must be more rattled than he wanted to let on if he kept repeating the same word. "We'll talk more when this is over."

"Sounds good to me," I replied before hanging up the phone.

I walked down the hallway until I reached the front desk, where I found an older gentleman sitting behind it, watching the local news, which was full of weather updates. It wasn't too late, but I imagined most everyone had either left or gone somewhere else to weather out the storm.

"I need another set of heavy drapes."

The man looked up at me, shaking his head. "We've taken all the extras we had to cover windows on the main floor."

"You got anyone staying on the upper floors?"

"Moved 'em all down to the ballroom. You should go there too."

"Give me a key to one of the upper rooms no one is in. I'll get the Goddamned curtains myself."

He blinked several times before shaking his head. "I can't do that, sir. I'm sorry. You should go to the ballroom with everyone else to wait out the storm."

With a growl, I turned and stomped away. I pulled out my phone and called Thorn.

"You guys OK?"

"Yeah. Tell Ripper I need an empty upper room opened. I need to get heavy drapes to protect us in case the windows break. Give us enough time to leave the room."

"Hang on."

There was some mumbling in the background, then Thorn called to Ripper.

"Phone. It's Ice. He needs your expertise."

"Hey, man. What do you need?"

"An empty room. Need to steal the drapes."

"Kind of an awkward and unusual theft, but I can dig it. You on the ground floor?"

"Yeah. Give me something above us. They've evacuated guests from the upper floors."

There were a couple beats of silence before Ripper answered me. "Second floor. Room two-two-seven. Should be close to the stairs. I've set an electronic key on the hotel's app. It'll be on your account."

"Thanks. What's the latest weather?" I talked to Ripper on the move. I didn't want to leave Dawn any longer than necessary. The storm wasn't bad yet, but it was picking up.

"The outer rain bands are overland now. Storm

surge is flooding lowlands next to the coast and expected to get worse as the storm progresses. It's expected to make landfall as a category three. Bad, but not as bad as it could be. You should be safe where you are."

As we talked, I took the stairs two at a time before jogging down the hall to the room Ripper had indicated. And thought, *This* is *pretty Goddamned bad*.

"Good. Let me know if they upgrade the storm or if we need to move."

"You just take care of El Diablo's daughter. Get through this storm, then take her home. That girl is his pride and joy. He and Jezebel have two other kids, but Dawn and that crazy fucker have a special relationship. Probably because she's his only daughter."

"Great," I muttered. "Sharing a room with the daughter of the world's deadliest assassin. Just fuckin' great."

"Yeah. Sucks to be you, Ice."

"Right. Sucks to be me."

Chapter Five

Dawn

I hated storms. Always did. Though, this was different. There was no thunder and lightning. Just howling wind and beating rain. Lots and lots of rain. I was bone-tired. Besides, having been driving for the better part of thirteen hours, the adrenaline had left me feeling nauseated and exhausted.

My phone rang. I glanced at the screen before closing my eyes and taking a shuddering breath. *David.* The last person on Earth I wanted to talk to. I let the call go to voicemail, but it immediately started ringing again.

"What do you want, David?"

"You to get your rich daddy to put more money in your bank account." He sounded so reasonable. Like he fully expected I'd just do what he told me.

"Have you lost your mind? I think you've stolen enough."

"You'll do it or I'll find you and kill everyone you've ever loved. Friends. Family. All gone."

"How you plan on doing that?"

"I got friends too, you know."

"You have no idea what you're getting yourself into."

David sounded calm, but I could hear a note of desperation in his voice.

"I know exactly what I'm getting myself into, Dawn." His tone turned dangerous. "And you know what's at stake here. Better get daddy to pony up the cash before it's too late."

"Look, David. Things ended badly between us, but I don't want you dead. That's exactly what will happen if you try to attack my family. My dad... he's not the kind of man you mess with."

"Forty-eight hours, Dawn. Then I'm coming for you."

The line went dead and I let out a long sigh.

"Fucking bastard."

I balled my hands into fists and tried to get my emotions under control. David was playing a dangerous game. And I had no idea what he was really up to. I didn't have feelings for the bastard. I meant it when I'd told Ice I was done with him. But I didn't want him to die.

"What's that?"

I jumped and squealed as the gruff voice came from the doorway between my and Ice's rooms.

"Jesus! Way to sneak up on a girl!"

"Sorry." He grinned. "Didn't mean to startle you." He pointed to the phone in my hand. "What was that?"

"Nothing." I turned away, tossing the phone to the bed. "Just bullshit."

"Uh-huh." I turned to move and the next thing I knew, Ice was snatching the phone from my bed. The screen hadn't locked, so he started looking through it.

"Give me that!" I grabbed for it, but he held it up out of my reach like I was a toddler or something.

"Nope. Not unless you want to tell me what had you calling someone a fucking bastard."

"Spam call," I snapped.

Then my phone dinged with a text message. Ice looked at me with a raised eyebrow.

"No! No, Ice. That's private."

"Who's David?" He hadn't opened the message, but the look on his face told me he suspected who he was.

"None of your business!"

"Oh?" He looked back at the phone and opened the message. I took a step back, knowing whatever David had sent wouldn't be good. Last thing I wanted was to get blowback from Ice's anger. Because I knew he'd be pissed.

Ice's face went cold. Like his namesake. He stared at the phone for so long I thought that maybe he couldn't read the message or was waiting for something.

"What does it say?" I asked quietly, feeling my stomach drop at the expression on his face.

"It's from David. He's threatening you." Ice's voice was low, dangerous. "This the guy you were dating?"

"If I say no, will you let it go?"

The last thing I expected was the reaction I got from Ice. With a yell, he threw my phone across the room, where it smashed into the wall. "He's fuckin' threatenin' you, Dawn! Threatenin' your family! And you were keeping this to yourself? What the fuck, Dawn?"

"It just happened! I haven't had a chance to tell anyone! Besides, he's a bastard, but I don't want him dead! I tell my dad and that's what happens. I won't have that on my conscience or my dad's." I'd taken a couple more steps back as I spoke. Logically, I knew Ice wouldn't hurt me, but the look on his face at the moment wasn't exactly encouraging.

"Trust me when I tell you, your dad wouldn't lose a moment's sleep over killin' this fuckin' punk. Neither would I." He pointed his finger to where the phone lay on the floor. "No one gets to talk to you that way, Dawn. Fuckin' nobody."

I looked up at him, unsure what to say. He stared at me, and I wasn't at all sure what was more intimidating. The storm outside or the one in my hotel room.

Ice scrubbed a hand over his face and turned away from me, rubbing his neck with his other hand as he did. He took several deep breaths before straightening and turning back to me.

"This guy hurt you, Dawn?"

I shook my head, not taking my eyes from Ice. "No."

"Dawn. Do *not* lie to me." He tilted his head giving me a warning look. "Tell me you don't want to answer or to kiss your ass or to go to hell, but you will not lie to me."

I shook my head and took another step back before putting my head up and standing my ground. "I don't answer to you. And I'm not about to give the bastard more money if that's what you're worried about."

"I could give a fuck about the money, Dawn. El Diablo won't either." He narrowed his eyes, and I knew I was fucking screwed. "It's more than just money. You could have called your dad and told him you needed more if it was just a matter of him taking what you had. Same with your credit card. You cancel it and have your dad get you a new one." He shook his head. "No. What else is fuckin' goin' on, Dawn?"

All I could do was shake my head. I wasn't telling him anything, but the look on his face and the cold rage in his eyes made me nearly as afraid of defying him as I was of staying in Kentucky. I trembled under his gaze. The rage. The way he towered over me. It was all too much, reminding me of...

A whimper escaped me, and I took several steps backward until I hit the vanity beside the bathroom.

"Hey, hey, hey. I'm sorry." Ice raised his hands and took a step backward himself. "I'm not gonna hurt you, honey. I didn't mean to scare you."

"I-I know." Before, when we were in the parking garage, I'd let out some of my fear, but there was so much more I'd locked inside me and it was in danger of escaping.

He shook his head. "Fuck. I've fucked this to shit and back." Ice took a careful step toward me. I cringed, but it was more reflex than anything else. The man was intimidating, but I'd grown up around intimidating men. It was only my recent experiences coloring my perception of him. I was back in my home territory. With men I was familiar with. Even if I didn't know Ice as well as the men in Black Reign and Salvation's Bane, Ice was just like them. They might skirt the law sometimes, but they all had a code of honor they followed. Ice would be no different or my father wouldn't have sent him after me.

"I'm sorry, Ice. I'm not afraid of you." I didn't move away from the counter, but I felt calmer. Just making myself remember who this man was, what he represented, helped to get myself under control.

"I'm coming closer." He paused a moment before taking a step toward me. Then another. The next thing I knew, he'd wrapped me up in his arms and my world seemed to right itself. "I'm so sorry, honey. Your dad'll have my balls for scarin' you like that."

"Yeah. I'll make sure to tell him about this first."

That got a deep chuckle from Ice that vibrated through my whole body. Big as he was, he surrounded me with his warmth and protection. I knew I was a job to him, but this represented the first time I'd felt truly safe in months. Since David had shown his true colors.

"OK, honey. Let's sit down and you can tell me

everything."

I snorted. "You think that's happening, but it's not."

"Yeah, it is. Because we've got hours before we can leave this hotel and I've got nothin' else to do but badger you until you talk." He picked me up then, carrying me to the bed where he sat us down with his back to the headboard and me sitting across his lap. I tried to move, but he just tightened his hold. "Nope. You're sittin' right here until we get all this out. Hear me?"

"You're not the boss of me, you know." But I honestly wasn't in any hurry to move.

"Keep tellin' yourself that, but I'm about to prove you wrong. I usually get what I want."

"Arrogant much?"

Again, he chuckled. I'd wanted to be angry at him for his highhandedness but couldn't. Being in his arms calmed me like nothing else in this world could have. I wasn't even sure being with my parents would have helped as much as this did. Not because I didn't trust them or love them. It was just… different.

"Yeah. My brothers at Bones say Arrogant is my middle name. Now. The quicker you get this out, the better you're gonna feel. Take a deep breath and start from the beginning."

* * *

Ice

Yep. I was fucking fucked. The reason I was fucking fucked was for several different reasons. First, this woman's tears and fear had the power to bring me to my knees even quicker than my mother's or sister's. Second, if this David character had caused her tears and fear, he was a dead-ass motherfucker. And third? I was a fucking dead man because when El Diablo figured out how much I wanted his daughter, he'd kill me slowly and painfully and I'd take it like a fucking man.

So, yeah. I was fucking fucked.

She looked up at me, her eyes wide. I could see her trying to decide what to do. Rather, trying to decide if she could out-stubborn me. I had news for her. She couldn't.

"Start talkin', honey."

At first, she lifted her chin again. Then, after staring up at me for a full minute, she seemed to deflate.

"David isn't... he's not a nice person. He singled me out because he thought I had money and because I got the better of him, but it's more than that."

When she stopped, I prodded her. "Keep going."

"He..." She trailed off, looking away. "He's mean."

"How?" I barked out the question that was more of a demand she tell me than an actual request.

"When I wouldn't sleep with him --" She closed her eyes as if trying to shut out the memory, and my stomach balled into a knot. Then she whispered. "He hit me."

I tightened my arms around her before I could stop myself. It wasn't much, but it was enough to register that she might be uncomfortable. Try as I might, though, I couldn't let her go. Taking several deep breaths, I tried to find some semblance of calm. And failed.

"What do you mean he fuckin' hit you?" I bit out each word through clenched teeth. I could tell she was disconcerted by my anger, but she didn't flinch or try to move out of my arms.

"Does it really matter? Just knowing he did is enough."

"No, it's not," I snapped. "I want to know every fuckin' detail of every second of everything he did to you, Dawn. Then there's gonna be a reckonin'."

"No, Ice. This is between me and you, or not at all. That's my condition."

"Why are you protecting this guy? Do you love him?"

"No. I'm protecting my dad."

"Fuck." I wrapped her up tighter in my arms. I was sure it had to be uncomfortable for her, but Dawn didn't say anything. In fact, she bunched her fist in my shirt and clung to me nearly as tightly as I clung to her. I tried to use that time to get myself under control. I needed to keep my wits about me for several reasons, not the least of which was the intensifying storm. I needed to be aware of everything, especially my phone in case Ripper needed to give me updates or a critical weather alert went out.

We sat there for a long while, the wind roaring outside and debris hitting the glass outside our room. Occasionally, Dawn would shiver, but she never tried to get up, seeming to take as much comfort from me as I needed to give to her. She seemed to have burrowed her face against my neck and stilled. I let her.

"This isn't over, honey." I didn't want to break the spell, but she had to know I was serious when I said I wanted to know what that son of a bitch had done to her. "You sit here as long as you need to, but we're gonna talk about this, and you're gonna give me what I want, Dawn. As to protecting your dad? He can take care of himself. They don't call him El Diablo for nothing. He didn't choose that name. The name chose him."

"It's not physically I'm talking about. I may not know everything about my father or his past life, but I know he was an assassin. I'd be naive if I thought he'd never kill again. But each kill had to take a little piece of his soul. David isn't worth chipping away another piece. And if Daddy knew he'd even used harsh language around me, he'd kill David. If he finds this out? Yeah. David would not only die, he'd die in the worst possible way El Diablo could manage."

I felt her shudder in my arms. She wasn't wrong. That's exactly what El Diablo would do.

"Honey, I think killin' someone like this guy would be doing humanity a service. El Diablo ain't gonna lose nothin' by killin' him. Even if he skinned the fucker alive. A man hurts a woman like that, he don't deserve to live."

She looked up at me then, meeting my gaze with sad eyes filled with tears she fought off bravely. "Maybe once he could have done it without it taking a piece of him, but Dad's not the same man he was before he met my mother and his daughter, Magenta. I've heard Rycks and El Segador talk about it. Samson too. They both gave him something that made him softer somehow but no less protective. Probably more protective than ever. Just telling him someone hit me might push him over the edge. I'm fine. I'm alive, I got away with just a few injuries, and I'm safe. Why torture my father with something he can't change that would only hurt him, my mom… all of us?"

"Fuck." Yeah. I was even more fucked than before. Because the next thing I knew, I was kissing Dawn. The daughter of the Devil.

She was still beneath my kiss. I felt her suck in a breath of surprise. Then she exhaled with a little sigh and just… surrendered to me. I grunted before deepening the kiss, sweeping my tongue over her lips gently until she opened her mouth and let me in.

Dawn was sweet as fuck, her whimpers and moans the sweetest music. She wiggled over my lap, turning more fully toward me as she slid her arms around my neck. There was no way she didn't feel my cock pressing against her hip, but she didn't seem to mind. In fact, she moved so that she straddled my hips, her knees on either side of me. The second she did that, she lowered herself so that my cock pressed between her legs.

Now it was my turn to shudder. She was so tiny in my arms. I wrapped her up and held her against me as I continued to kiss her, holding her to me. Afraid she'd somehow slip away from me. I'd known I wanted her before, but something inside me woke up. Like she'd flipped some kind of switch that I could never turn back off. From this moment forward, Dawn was mine. I knew it like I knew my own name. I would claim her. Then I'd slay her demons. Once that was done, I'd make her my woman forever.

I rolled us so that I was over Dawn. She wrapped her legs around my waist, clinging to me with everything she had. All the while, she let me kiss her. She even kissed me back, her little tongue darting inside my mouth to lap at mine. I thrust against her, wanting to see what she'd do. How she'd respond.

The second I contacted her clit through her clothing, she stiffened, then cried out, arching her back and digging her heels into the backs of my thighs.

"Ice!" She gasped my name, her eyes wide in surprise and maybe a hint of fear. "What is this?"

"Just relax, baby. Don't fight it. Embrace it."

The second the words left my mouth, Dawn nodded, then her body jerked. Then she opened her mouth and screamed. She threw her head back, giving me access to her neck, which I eagerly took. I kissed and nipped at the tender skin I found, needing to draw out her orgasm as long as I could. Much as I wanted to, I couldn't fuck her. Not now. She trusted me in a sense, but she didn't know me. Not yet.

Before long, Dawn's cries had turned to soft moans and sobs. Her breathing came out in little ragged puffs as I finally loosened my death grip on her. I still held her close to me, relishing the feeling of her lush, soft body against my larger, harder one.

I kissed her temple and murmured soft nonsense to her, trying to bring her down gently as her climax faded.

"That's it, baby. Just breathe through it. I've got you. I'm not going anywhere."

"Ice." My name on her lips in that breathy whisper made my cock ache to fill her. I wanted her like I wanted my next breath. But I knew if I made love with her now, it would be a mistake. She wasn't ready. Not while she still kept secrets from me.

"I'm right here, baby." I stroked her hair away from her face as she looked up at me. Tears streaked down her temples, but she gazed up at me with a look of wonder on her lovely face.

"I've never felt anything like that before."

I leaned down to kiss her chin. Then her nose. Then each of her eyes. "You said you weren't ready to sleep with David. That you knew it wouldn't be him. Have you ever had sex before, Dawn?"

She shook her head slightly. "No."

"Has a guy ever made you come?" Again she shook her head. "What about on your own? You touch yourself?"

"Yeah. At least, I thought I had." She shook her

head again. "But nothing like that. Never."

"Good. Thank you for giving this to me, Dawn. It's a gift I'll always treasure."

A confused look came over her face, but I didn't expect what she said next. "Are you sure you're a biker?"

I barked out a laugh. "Pretty sure. But why do you ask?"

"'Cause I've never heard any of the bikers I've been around talk like that. It was almost poetic."

"Blame my mom. She's a teacher."

Finally, *finally*! For the first time since I'd found Dawn in this fucking storm, she gave me a genuine, happy, *glorious* smile. Her hand came up to my face to stroke my beard and she pulled me back to her, kissing me so fucking sweetly.

"Thank you, Ice. That was the most wonderful experience of my life."

"So far." I gave her a wink. "Now. Much as I'd love to explore that sexy little body of yours, you've distracted me long enough." I gave her what I hoped was a stern look but wasn't sure I quite pulled it off. "Tell me about your time with this David guy."

Chapter Six

Dawn

This was going to happen. I didn't want to talk about it, but Ice was going to get this out of me. I knew that. The only question was did I try to fight it or surrender and let him know the power he had over me? I wasn't sure why we'd just shared what we had -- Ice hadn't come or even tried to do anything more with me -- but I knew I'd already given him more than I should have. Yet, I was giving him more. I knew I was.

"I don't really know where to start."

"How about from the beginning, honey. Always a great place to start." He grinned at me as he pushed himself off me. If I thought he was going to give me a reprieve, I was wrong. Ice sat back against the headboard again, pulling me onto his lap once again. This time, however, he had me facing him, his hands on my hips.

With a heavy sigh, I began. "I have no idea why I chose the University of Kentucky to go to school. I wasn't going into medicine and I wasn't good at sports of any kind. But I loved Lexington and UK is only an hour and a half from Somerset. I was close to a club my dad trusted but still away from home so I could... I don't know. *Not* be El Diablo's daughter? No one in Kentucky other than Bones knew who Black Reign and El Diablo were."

"So you wanted to be more than your father's daughter."

"Exactly! I love my dad, but I needed to get out from under his umbrella."

He smiled at me. "I hear you. Go on."

"Well, I wanted to teach math in high school. So, my adviser loaded my schedule with a pretty full first, then second, semester. That was when I met David. He was in one of the calculus classes I was taking. We went out a couple of times before things started to get a little intense."

"What do you mean by intense?"

I shrugged. "He started pushing me to have sex and I didn't want to."

"That when he hit you?"

"No. That came later. I said he hit me when I wouldn't have sex with him, but I honestly think it was more than that. I had a better grade than him at the midterm. But it wasn't just that. More than one of my projects got the highest score in a class of over fifty students. David was consistently in the bottom third."

"So, he couldn't handle you outperforming him."

"That's what I think. After our grades came in at the midterm, he followed me to my dorm. He'd walked me up several times before so it wasn't anything unusual. But when we got there and my roommate wasn't there, he forced his way inside and told me he was tired of waiting. I refused, fighting him as hard as I could. He backhanded me." I wanted to stop there, hoping I'd given him enough of my story he'd think that was it.

Ice was silent for a moment, looking at me steadily. It was like he was trying to see inside my head to my memories of that day while I tried desperately to keep him out.

"What else happened, Dawn? Tell me the rest of it."

"That's it." I bit my lip, looking away. Yeah. I was a horrible liar.

"What did I tell you about lying to me?"

"I don't want to tell you."

"Tough."

"Kiss my ass?"

His lips twitched. "Yeah. Happily. But you're still gonna tell me what that son of a bitch did."

I sighed, defeated. I knew I wasn't going to win this one. "I really don't want to talk about it, Ice. But..." I closed my eyes and turned my head. I could feel tears burning and my throat closing. "It was the worst night of my life. He knew what he was doing because not one single blow landed where anyone could readily see, so I'm pretty sure he's done it before." I took a deep breath. Though I'd changed out of my wet clothes with him right behind me, Ice had been very careful to keep his back to me and I'd been careful to make sure he was being careful. It wasn't because I was modest.

Slowly, so Ice could stop me if he wanted to -- giving me the excuse I needed not tell him -- I pulled my shirt over my head before laying it down beside me. I could feel his gaze moving over me like a burning flame. I knew what my torso looked like. It was mottled with bruises. My hips and upper thighs were as well, though he couldn't see them. Yet.

I tried to avoid looking at Ice, but as the silence dragged on, I had to. His cold green gaze moved over my body, his expression growing more and more thunderous as the seconds ticked by.

"How much of this is from you getting knocked around when your car got pushed around?"

"I don't know." My voice sounded small and unsure. I had no idea how to deal with this. I wasn't what I'd consider a strong woman. At least not when faced with evidence of this abuse.

"I'm guessing not much since what I can see looks like the bruising has mostly turned purple with no red, so at least a couple days old." He lifted me off his lap so I stood beside the bed. "Take the rest of it off, Dawn."

"What?" I squeaked out my question. I'd never been naked in front of a man in my life! And I was supposed to do this now? When instead of seeing me as a woman he wanted to have sex with, this man who'd just given me the most intense pleasure of my life wanted me naked so he could see me as a victim? To see my humiliation? "No!"

"Dawn, I'm going to see you naked eventually. I confess, this isn't exactly what I had in mind, but I'm gonna see the rest of the damage that bastard did. Then we'll decide what to do from there."

"What do you mean, decide what to do?"

"Honey, some of these bruises look like they're over something important. You need a doc to look you over."

"Well, we don't have one here."

"No, but your club has one. So does mine. Bane does as well. If nothing else, one of them needs to have a look and decide if you need more direct medical care."

"And have them go straight to my father? No, Ice. No fucking way."

"How about this -- Mama's our club doc. She was a surgeon in another life, or so my dad tells me. She has her own secrets to keep so she'll understand. I can hook you up on Facetime with her and the two of you can talk privately."

My instinct was to shake my head and deny him, but I figured he'd just keep at me until he got what he wanted. "Fine. But I want your word and hers that no one will go to my father with this. I'll take care of David on my own."

"You don't really expect me to let this go. Do

you?"

"You? Why would you care as long as he doesn't hurt me again?"

He pulled me closer to him, so I was standing between his legs with his hands on my hips. "Honey. Do you honestly think I'd share something with you as intimate as what we just did if I didn't intend to keep you?"

That shocked me. "Keep me? What does that mean?"

"You know what it means. You're the daughter of another MC president. A very dangerous one. I'm not stupid enough to let something like that just happen. Your father would have my balls, and he'd make me cut them off myself. I didn't set out to find you with the intention of makin' you mine, but the second I saw you I knew it was only a matter of time."

I looked up at him. Even sitting on the bed in front of me, he still seemed to loom over me. Maybe it was because Ice was so larger than life. My hero. Literally. All I knew was the thought of belonging to this man was as intimidating as it was thrilling.

"But my father --"

"Will respect my claim if I do right by you. That includes finding this bastard and makin' sure he pays for what he did."

I bit my lip, looking away from him. I didn't want to agree. Didn't want anyone to see me like this, least of all Ice. Even now, I covered up my breasts with my arms over my chest, but Ice gently grasped my wrist.

"No, Dawn. Don't cover yourself from me. I'm the man who gets to see every part of you, no matter what. We don't hide from each other."

"That's easy for you. You're not the one standing

here battered and broken." I couldn't keep the sob out of my voice or the tears from tracking down my cheeks. "I've never been so humiliated in my life." My voice was a mere whisper of sound. I was surprised he heard me, but Ice grasped my chin firmly but gently and forced me to look at him.

"I'm not judging you if that's what you think. I'm sitting here plotting how best to keep that fucker alive long enough to make him hurt like he hurt you."

With a sigh, I nodded. "OK. But I'm not promising to go to the doctor or hospital. No matter what she says. I'm not getting the police involved."

He gave me an annoyed look. "What part of this do you think I'd let the police get involved in?"

"Poor choice of words. I've been thinking like a civilian instead of the daughter of an MC president, I guess."

"That stops now, honey. You were taken into this life by your father when you were little more than a toddler. In a situation like this? Use that advantage he gave you. If not for yourself, then for the next woman he tries to do this to."

How could this man know me so well already? He'd only been around me a few hours, yet he had to know I'd never turn David over to him or my father for myself. For another woman, though... What if it had been Tabitha or Holly? OK, so Holly would have already killed the motherfucker, but what if?

"You're right. If I can't do it for myself, I should do it for the other girls in Black Reign."

Ice gave me a crisp nod. "Good. Now. Before I call Mama, we need to finish this." He nodded to my shorts. "Off."

"I don't have on any underwear, Ice!"

"And I'm gonna see it all eventually. I promise I

won't jump on you yet." He gave me a gentle smile. His words were teasing, but I could see the strain around his eyes and his mouth. He was trying to lighten the mood, but I could see he was feeling anything but lighthearted. "Come on. Let's get this done."

With a little whimper, I pulled at the string holding the shorts around my waist. Gently, Ice turned me around, inspecting my body as he went. I knew what I looked like because I'd stood in front of the mirror the day I'd left, trying to make sure all the visible injuries on my body were covered by my clothing. Anyone with any experience could look at the shape of the bruising on my body and tell I'd been beaten up. Finger marks and fist-sized contusions, as well as a tread print, were all over me. The only place spared was my face.

Ice turned me around and met my gaze with a hard one of his own. "I swear to you, Dawn. I'm gonna kill this son of a bitch." He gripped my upper arms gently. Just enough to hold me still while he made his solemn vow.

"I don't want that." My voice was soft. Meek. "Not because of me."

"Then I'll do it so no one else suffers what you have if that makes you feel better. But he's gonna die."

Hadn't I just been thinking about Tabitha and Holly? I knew this had to happen, but I didn't want it to. "Sometimes, I wish I could deal with things in the normal way. There probably wouldn't be as much done or much resolution, but being judge, jury, and executioner has to take a toll. I don't want to contribute to someone losing their humanity."

"Has that happened to your father? Do you feel like he's lost something that makes him care about people? Your mother? You?"

"What? No!" I shook my head sharply. "I know my dad loves me. He shows me every day. I see how much he loves my mother too. All the kids at Reign. My dad has a bigger heart than he wants anyone to know, but he's also the coldest killer. I don't ever want that side to overshadow the man who loves his family so much."

"As much as he's killed, Dawn, if he were going to lose his humanity or his capacity to love, he'd have already done it. And maybe he had before he found his eldest daughter or your mother. No. He kills to keep his family safe. And not indiscriminately. Sure, he may threaten a prospect if he looks at one of you girls the wrong way or the boys if they make you cry, but he'd never really do it. For something like this, though --" He waved his hand down my body. "-- He'd do it without a moment's regret and consider it his privilege. Anyone who'd do this to you or any other woman deserves nothing less."

Ice gripped my hips gently and pulled me closer to him. I stood between his legs, inches from him. His hands stroked up my sides once, then back to my hips. The look on his face was a mixture of lust and anger so fierce I wasn't sure what to make of it.

"You're so Goddamned beautiful it hurts, Dawn." His voice was a husky whisper. "So Goddamned beautiful…"

He moved his hands to cup my face before leaning in to kiss me gently. I closed my eyes in bliss for the few seconds he lingered. I know when he pulled back there was a dreamy smile on my face.

"That's a look I hope to always keep on your face." I opened my eyes to find him looking at me with a soft, almost loving, expression. "Now. We'll Facetime

Mama. The storm's getting worse, and I have no idea how long we have before we lose regular cell service. We need to do this now, so I know if it's safe to wait here with you."

"I mean, can we even go anywhere now?"

"If we have to, I'll find a way, honey. I'll make it happen. Storm be damned."

"God, you're so much like my father." I couldn't help but smile. "That's exactly something he'd say and he'd mean it. Nothing or no one will stand in the way of him making sure the people he loves are safe."

"And that's why he'll agree with me this fucker David needs to die. You got a last name for me? I'll take this to Zora and Suzie instead of Data if you like. That way it has a woman's touch instead of a bulldozers." His smile took some of the weight of the situation from me, but there was still deadly intent there. It was a look I'd seen my father use on more than one occasion. Usually when someone was in deep trouble and he was trying to soften the blow.

"Almond. David Almond."

"See? That wasn't so hard."

"I feel like I've just signed his death warrant. I don't want to be the one to do that."

"You're not, honey. And if you think I'll do this arbitrarily, you'd be mistaken. I might not hesitate to kill the bastard if I caught him in the act, but the reason I'm bringing in my intel people is not just to find him, but to look into his life. You said you thought he knew what he was doing because any damage he did wasn't readily visible. I intend to find out if that's so. Also, I intend to put the full weight of my club behind this. They'd all agree his life is forfeit after what he did to you, but we like to prove a pattern. Call it justification for something we want to do if you want. And maybe that's what it is. But this fucker's gonna die. How hard depends on what we find."

I smiled and shook my head, knowing there was no way I was talking him out of this. Hell, I wasn't sure I really wanted to. "I guess this is one of the many reasons my dad liked the connection to Bones. You and Bane are exactly like Reign. Maybe it *is* all about justification, but there's always a good reason to punish someone when you do it."

"We don't hurt people for the fuck of it, honey. You already know that. I could do this for the simple fact that you're El Diablo's daughter, but I'm not. I want my club firmly on board because I'm doing this because you're my woman. Fuck El Diablo."

I raised an eyebrow even as I had to fight another grin. "You gonna tell him that?"

He barked out a laugh. "No. I'm crazy. Not stupid."

Chapter Seven

Ice

I initiated the call with Mama, telling her what I needed then left her and Dawn alone to talk. I knew if anyone could get the truth out of her it would be Mama. She'd been a driving force in Bones far longer than I'd been alive, but she always knew when to use a firm or a gentle touch. I shut the connecting door to my room to give them some privacy, but I hated it. I didn't like anything between us. Not even a closed door. And it was way too fucking early in this to be this possessive. To pass the time, I called Ripper for an updated weather report.

"Gettin' bad. It picked up steam just before it brushed land. We're still on the fringe. Been a category three this whole time, but it just increased to a cat four. And it's stalled. Which means more rain which means more surge. Water every-fucking-where."

"Do we need to leave our room? Go to the hotel storm shelter -- which is the ball room on the inner first floor."

"Up to you. Though, if you stay in your room, I'd commandeer more than a heavy set of drapes. Get a couple mattresses, too. Use the same room you took the drapes from."

"Copy that."

"How she holdin' up?"

"Yeah... She's good." I had to be careful here. I made promises to Dawn I intended to keep, but lying to my sister club didn't sit right with me. "There's some... issues. I'll deal with them on my end, but I may need some backup."

"Hang on."

There was silence for a few moments until

Ripper gave the phone to Thorn.

"What's going on?" It was a demand more than a question, and it took everything inside me not to immediately fork over the information. Thorn was no longer my superior. I was his equal now. President of Bones. Instead of telling him to mind his own fucking business, however, I did my best to soften the blow while still getting my point across.

"Nothing you need to worry about yet. I'll give you plenty of heads-up if I need assistance. Just know there are extenuating circumstances."

"She good?"

"For now. I'll let you know if that changes."

There was a pause as Thorn moved. I could hear background noise around him. Men talking. Women. Then a door shut and the noise was gone. I heard a chair squeak as Thorn must have sat.

"What the fuck's goin' on, Ice?"

"Nothing I can't handle."

"Not good enough!" he snapped. "This is El Diablo's daughter we're talkin' about."

"Believe me, Thorn. Of all the things I'm oblivious to, the fact that I've got the Devil's daughter in my care isn't one of them." Respect only went so far. While I admired Thorn and all he'd done for ExFil and Salvation's Bane, he didn't get to order me around. I wasn't patched into Bane, and he definitely wasn't my president. I'd still answer to Cain but only because he was my former president and boss as well as my father. "I wouldn't have mentioned anything at all, but I didn't want to blindside you. And I absolutely will not take chances with her."

"Good. Then you'll tell me what the fuck's goin' on." There was steel in his voice. I didn't like it.

"Thorn, you're one of my dad's oldest friends,

and I appreciate all you've done for him both in the club and with ExFil. But you don't get to demand shit from me."

"I do when you're performing a service in my fuckin' name."

"Tell El Diablo I've gone rogue. Whatever you like that will let you off the hook. His daughter told me something in confidence, and I'm not breaking that trust unless it's life or death. I realize it's a shit move to tell you there might be a problem, then not give you all the information, but this girl is in my care. I'll make the decisions I need to, to keep her safe and bring her back to her father. Besides, I can handle this myself without incident. I only mentioned it so I don't get caught flat-footed."

"You better be right about this, Ice."

"If I'm not, I'll eat crow and beg you for your help. Ain't too proud to admit when I'm wrong."

"Fine." He sighed. "You're just like your old man, you know. You might not be his biological child, but I can see his influence in your upbringing every fuckin' time I'm around you."

"Gonna take that as a compliment whether you mean it or not."

"It is. Good luck, brother. Keep our girl safe."

"Fully intend to."

My next call was to my sister, Suzie.

"Hey, Cliff! When you coming home? You're being safe right?"

"Hey, Suz. Yeah. Being as careful as I can be. I need a favor. Can you help me out?"

"You know I can. What do you need?"

Me, Daniel, and Suzie were all adopted by Cain when we were young teens. Suzie was even younger. We'd been in the foster system together since Suzie was six. Daniel was my biological brother, but Suzie had latched on to us almost from the moment we saw her. She was the most beautiful little girl I'd ever seen and the two of us had taken her under our wings. The home we were in was shit. The couple was more interested in the government payout for keeping foster kids than they were in taking care of us. So the three of us split.

Things hadn't turned out so well for us in the beginning, and we'd gotten into a hell of a situation, but we'd protected Suzie and eventually fled to Bones where Cain and Angel had adopted us. Suzie had eventually married Stunner, the man who'd watched over us when things had gone south and pointed us in the direction of Bones. That hadn't been a smooth transition for him and Cain, but they'd managed. Now, Suzie and Stunner were responsible for the grandchild Cain wanted to spend more time with. And I adored my niece as much as I adored Suzie.

"I need you to look into someone for me. Discreetly. Use Zora if you need to, but don't involve Data unless you absolutely need his help. It's not got anything to do with trust, I just promised I'd keep this between you ladies."

"This sounds serious. You OK?" Of course, Suzie was worried. When she loved, she loved with her whole heart. There was never any doubt that my sister loved me and my brother.

"I'm fine, Suz. Promise. I've got a… friend who might not be, though."

"You got a name?"

"Yeah. David Almond. I want to know everything shady you can find on him. Specifically, any women he's been with. And if they had any problems. I also want to know his current location."

"On it."

"Mum's the word, Suz. Keep it on the DL. Get me?"

"I promise. I'll only bring in Zora if I get stuck. I'll contact you before I involve Data."

"You're the best. How's my niece?"

"A little angel," she said with obvious affection in her voice. "You know. Now that she's asleep."

I barked out a laugh. "Yeah, that one's gonna be a hellion."

"Be safe, Cliff. Promise me."

"I promise. Let me know when you have something."

"Love you, big brother!"

"Love you too, pipsqueak."

I ended the call and took a deep breath. The next call I needed to make was probably going to get me killed, but I had to do it. Taking a deep breath, I made the call to El Diablo.

"Is my daughter OK?"

"Yes, sir. She's safe. I'm keeping us in the rooms Ripper got for us and have hung a second layer of heavy drapes on the windows, but I'll be putting mattresses over the windows as well. If it gets too bad, we'll go to the hotel ballroom. They've set it up as a storm shelter. I'd prefer to keep her away from everyone if I can, though."

There was a deep sigh on the other end. "Good. That's good." He sounded more like a worried father than an assassin at the moment, but I never forgot he was the latter. "You take care of my baby girl, Ice. You hear me?"

"I will. There's something else I need to discuss with you. About Dawn."

There was silence and I could almost feel the

man putting two and two together. There was no way he could know my feelings for his daughter since even I hadn't known, so hopefully what he came up with was way worse than me falling for Dawn.

"You said she was OK. Right?"

"She is. Safe in our rooms where I hope we can stay until the storm passes."

"I see." The man was making me nervous. He acted like he knew something, but there was no way he could. Or maybe it was just my guilty conscience. While I had every intention of making Dawn my woman, telling her father -- who was literally the Devil -- took every ounce of testicular fortitude inside me.

"Look. There's no subtle way to bring this up, but it has to be done now. Dawn's mine. I'm makin' her my old lady the second we get back to Kentucky."

There was a long silence. One I didn't dare break. I might have just signed my own death warrant, but I could honestly say the words felt right. Dawn *was* going to be my woman. Which meant El Diablo was… going to be my fucking father-in-law. Great. Fucking fantastic.

"You sound pretty sure of yourself. Have you taken advantage of my daughter, you son of a bitch?"

I'd spoken with El Diablo many times over the years. He was always immaculate and fully in control. Even when he sounded mad, it was more to elicit a certain action from someone than to show real anger. Today, I'd heard two emotions from El Diablo. Fear when he asked Thorn for help. Now, I heard true, unadulterated anger. Yeah. El Diablo wasn't happy at all that I'd set my sights on his eldest daughter.

"I think you know I'd never do anything to hurt her. And really. With a daddy named the Devil, why would I tell you this if I wasn't sure of my feelings for her and her feelings for me?"

"We'll talk about this later, Ice." El Diablo's voice was low and deadly. The assassin. "Right now, you concentrate on keeping Dawn safe. Then bring her home to me. Not to your club in Kentucky."

"I'll bring her home to get her things, but she's coming back with me."

"Like I said. Not. Now." He ended the call.

"Well, that went well." Christmas was gonna be a field day this year.

Chapter Eight

Dawn

The call with Mama was both comforting and uncomfortable. Given the attack had happened a couple of days prior and I wasn't having increasing pain, she thought I'd be fine until the storm passed. She was not happy with the fact that David was still alive and able to hurt me or someone else.

While I had her there, I asked about Ice. "He saved me, Mama. He was patient and careful, but he got me out of a bad situation and to safety. Not only that, but he didn't tell me how stupid I was to try to make it home during a hurricane. And that was before he knew why."

"I can see you like him." The older woman smiled at me. She had tanned, weathered skin and long, stark white hair. She was thin but fit, with eyes as hard as any MC president. She was a woman not to be fucked with. "Is it hero worship?"

"Maybe. I'm not going to deny that. Which is why I'm asking you about him. My dad always says you and Pops were the most honorable people he knows. Is Ice a good man?"

"I love that boy and his brother and sister like they were my own." Mama smiled fondly. "But you're right. I'd tell you if he wasn't a good man. No worries there. He'll be faithful and good to you. Most of all, he'll protect you ruthlessly. So I'm going to give you two pieces of vital information." She leaned in close to the camera. "First, he will absolutely do everything in his power to keep you happy. He learned that from Cain when he found Angel. Over the years, both Cliff and Daniel have watched how he treats his wife and followed his lead, coddling and protecting both Angel and Suzie as best they could as children, then even better as they grew into the men they are today.

"Second -- and this may be the more difficult one for you -- if he feels like he needs to avenge you, let him. Trust him to know how far is too far. He'll see hunting down your attacker as protecting you, and that's something that's ingrained into his being." She smiled but I got the sense it was in pride for Ice and his brother, Cyclone.

"Those two boys brought Suzie to us when they were barely more than boys themselves. Did you know they pretended to do poorly in school when Angel was their teacher just so Suzie would do better than them? All so little Suzie could build her self-esteem. By doing better in school than either of them, they thought she'd feel like she'd accomplished something special. They were right. Though, it didn't take long for her to really be doing better than the two of them."

"Wow. That's so caring of them."

"They're extraordinary men, Dawn. Just like other men their age, they've not lived like monks. They take their pleasures, and often. But if Ice has committed to you, he'll be faithful. Love will come later because you won't be able to help yourself and neither will he."

I smiled, feeling even more at ease than before. "Now I just have to convince my father. He's not going to like this."

"El Diablo will come around," Mama said with a snort. She frowned. "If not, you come to me. I'll set him straight."

"You're probably the only person I've ever met who's not intimidated by my father."

"El Diablo is a formidable opponent. I'd be remiss if I didn't consider him as such. But he doesn't kill indiscriminately. In fact, he's painstakingly careful to not kill someone who doesn't deserve killing. Like Magenta's mother, Ginger. She tried to get him to kill her parents, saying they were abusing both her and Magenta. His first instinct was to protect his daughter, but he investigated the matter and found it was Ginger who was the problem. So, I respect him. But he doesn't intimidate me. Besides, I knew him before he was El Diablo."

"I hope you're right."

"Trust me on this one, sweetheart." With one last, encouraging smile, Mama disconnected the call.

I sat on the bed for a long time, trying to process everything that had happened in the last few hours. I was exhausted but so jittery I knew I'd never be able to sleep.

The wind was raging outside, having picked up even more. I wanted to check the progress of the storm on my phone, but I also didn't want to use any more of my phone's battery than I had to. I had it on the charger where I intended for it to stay until the storm passed or the electricity went out. I didn't figure it mattered much anyway. Ice was probably getting all that information while he waited on me to finish with Mama. I also had to wonder if he'd kept his end of the bargain and not told my father or anyone else what had happened. Because I knew he'd have to talk to my father now that we were settled in for the duration.

I'm not sure how long I sat there, trying to breathe through the adrenaline let-down. When the knock came at the door to the adjoining room with Ice, I wasn't really surprised. I took several deep breaths, trying to find the strength to stand. I was still shaking -- the call with Mama brought back a lot of memories. The storm was only one small part of it. The beating I'd taken from David had been debilitating. Having to relive it with Mama had been the worst kind of brutal. There were several times I thought I might have to stop the questioning but managed to power through. Now I was completely drained.

"Dawn? You good?"

God, I loved Ice's voice. I could just sit and listen to him for hours. Days. Hearing that low rumble of his voice settled something inside me like nothing else ever had. I let out a breath I hadn't even known I'd been holding.

"Yes. You can come in."

He hesitantly cracked the door open just a touch until he saw me sitting on the bed. Then he opened it and stepped all the way inside.

"Honey, you're trembling."

I tried to smile but wasn't sure I managed. "Adrenaline let-down. Going through everything with Mama was... difficult."

He sighed, stepping closer to me. "I'm sorry, honey. But you know it had to be done. I won't risk you being hurt without getting some kind of medical care. She say you need to go to the hospital?"

"No. She said since it had been a couple of days and I wasn't having increasing pain that I'd probably be OK until the storm passed. I'm supposed to call her if there is more pain or any bleeding."

"How is your pain?"

"Surprisingly good. Sure, there's some, but not nearly as much as the day right after it happened. Nothing lingering that's not showing improvement."

"Good." He knelt in front of me. "I've got some mattresses to put over the windows, as well as a couple to protect you while you sleep."

"Won't you be sleeping too? I mean, I thought..."

"Yeah, honey. I'll lie with you while you sleep, but I'll likely doze at best. I'm a little on edge with the storm." He smiled as he reached up to brush a lock of hair off my forehead. "I like the position of the bed to the window better in my room than here. I think I can better protect you in there. You good with me staying with you?"

"You know I am. It's what I want most right now." It was. I don't think I'd even latched on to my mom and dad as quickly as I had Ice. "Maybe it's just this whole situation combined with what we shared earlier, but I don't want to separate from you."

"You won't. We're in this together." He framed my face with his hands before pulling me down slightly for a soft kiss. He didn't linger more than a couple seconds before he stood, holding his hand out to me. "Come on. Let's get settled and get some rest. If nothing goes wrong, we can hole up here until the storm passes. Ripper thinks it could be as long as twenty-four hours. The only question is if we get flooded out. I think we're good, but I'm keeping an eye on it. Ripper has real-time satellite imagery watching us like a hawk. If the storm surge looks like it's going to get too bad, he'll tell us where we need to go."

"Did you talk to my father?"

He grunted. I could tell by the tight expression on his face that conversation hadn't gone well. "Yeah. I'm not borrowing trouble, Dawn. I'll get you through this safely, then I'll deal with El Diablo."

The thought my dad wouldn't approve of me being with Ice hurt something deep inside me. Could I go against him if he told me not to be with Ice? Would Ice go against him?

"Hey, what did I just say?" He stroked my cheek with his thumb where he still framed my face with his hands. His voice was gentle but firm. "Don't borrow trouble."

"But what if he doesn't want me with you?"

To my surprise, Ice smiled. "Baby, if El Diablo ever approves of me being with his beloved daughter, I'll be surprised. He's the Devil. There isn't a man on the planet he'd think could protect you better than him. Ain't sayin' I can, but I will cherish you and we will grow to love each other madly."

I whimpered before throwing myself into his arms, wrapping myself around him and holding on for dear life. Ice sat on the floor and held me as tightly as I held him. He soothed me with tender words while he rubbed my back up and down in relaxing strokes until I finally relaxed fully against him.

"It's going to be fine, honey. I won't let it be anything else."

"Make love to me, Ice." No one was more surprised by my whispered plea than me. Is that really what I wanted?

Yeah. I couldn't think of anything in that moment I wanted more than for Ice to make love to me.

"Be very sure, Dawn. I'm not taking your virginity only to give you up to the next guy who rescues you in a hurricane." He grinned, but I knew what he meant.

"I wouldn't have asked if I didn't mean to stay with you. Mama says you're a good man. My dad trusts her more than just about anyone so I'm going to trust her too. She says to let you take care of everything, that you'll be good to me."

"She's not wrong. Once we commit to each other, that's it. I'll be yours and you'll be mine. We make this work between us and live happily ever after."

I couldn't help but grin. "Happily ever after, huh?"

His lips quirked up on one side. "Yeah. Happily ever fuckin' after."

"OK, then. Because that's what I want. I just never thought I'd have it."

"Why?" He tilted his head to the side, genuinely curious.

"Because of my dad. You're right. He's never going to be satisfied with any man I want to date."

"Good thing we're not datin' then, huh?"

"We're not?"

"Oh no, baby. This isn't me datin' you. This is me claiming you for my own."

"Then I'm claiming you as well."

"Pretty sure that's the way it goes." He grinned. Then he fisted his hand in the hair at the back of my head before kissing me.

There wasn't pain so much as a slight sting where he moved my head with my hair. Surprisingly, the little bite of pain only made things that much more intense. I moaned as he kissed me with wicked strokes of his tongue. It wasn't long before I found myself giving as good as I was getting.

"So fuckin' sweet. I'm gonna make you so fuckin' happy, Dawn. Give you more fuckin' pleasure than you ever dreamed."

"Ice…"

He kissed me again, wrapping me up tighter while he stood and carried me to his room. The next thing I knew, he'd laid me on the bed and covered me with his own large frame. I hugged his hips with my thighs as I looked up into his rugged, handsome face.

"This only goes as far as you want, honey." He gently stroked my face before leaning in to kiss my chin. "If you get scared or just change your mind, you can always stop me."

I shook my head. "Don't want to stop you. I want this. I want you."

He gave me a sexy smirk. "Good."

Then he was kissing me again.

The wind raged outside, the windows rattled as debris pelted the hotel, but all I cared about was the sounds coming from this man as he grunted his approval when I surrendered to him.

I loved the feel of his arms winding around me, holding me to him. The way his body mashed so securely against mine. His weight was heavy, pressing me into the mattress, but it was a comforting weight. I knew beyond any doubt that Ice would protect me from anything. The storm. David. Even my father if he thought he had to. And he might just. Not that I believed my dad would hurt me or anything, but if he tried to make Ice leave me, I'd be devastated.

He made his way from my mouth to the column of my neck, kissing and nipping the whole way. I shivered, whimpering as he kissed my collarbone and nudged the T-shirt neck out of his way to go lower.

"Need to lose this shirt, baby. Objections?"

I shook my head. When he pushed his weight off me, I tried to shimmy out of the shirt, but it got stuck between my back and the mattress. My mind was such a muddled mess of lust and need, I couldn't seem to figure out how to get the fucking thing off!

His warm chuckle should have offended me, but when I saw his cock proudly tenting his shorts, all I could do was stare at him with my mouth watering. "Let me help you." Instead of pulling it all the way off, he shoved it up over my bare breasts before he froze. "Fuck... me..." He scrubbed a hand over his mouth, his gaze zeroing in on my breasts.

Before I could ask what was wrong, he let out what sounded like a defeated groan and latched on to one nipple with his mouth, sucking strongly. I cried out, my hands going to his hair. I'd intended on pushing him away but ended up wrapping my arms around his head and holding him to me tightly.

He grunted before sliding down my body -- still latched on to my nipple -- and wrapped his arms around me once again while he feasted.

I think he took my whole breast into his mouth while he flicked and licked my hard peak only to occasionally suck it before he moved to the other side. He lavished the same attention on that breast, his short beard abrading my sensitive skin in the most tantalizing way. The more he did it, the more out of control I felt. My pussy clenched and my clit ached and throbbed where it brushed lightly against his stomach through my shorts.

Vaguely, I could hear the wind picking up, but it might have been the roaring in my ears as Ice continued to drive me higher and higher. The pleasure was indescribable! Was sex always like this? Is this what I'd been missing out on by not sleeping with David?

No. I knew that with absolute certainty the second the question popped into my head because I'd never had this level of attraction to David. Not in any way. Maybe it was the danger we'd faced together. The way he'd protected me and helped me. Kept me centered. All I knew was I was absolutely certain that, if Ice didn't fuck me right here and now, I would die. Simple as that. Something inside me would explode and I'd die right fucking here.

"Ice! Oh, God!"

"Fuck, baby! Fuck!"

He scrambled to his knees and grasped the waist of my shorts, pulling them down my hips in sharp, jerky motions. The look on his face was of barely controlled lust. I could actually see the effort it took for him to remove my clothing before pouncing on me. He looked like he wanted to just shove the too-large leg opening to the side and push inside me. Which, I wasn't too proud to admit, I wouldn't have objected to.

"Need you naked. Right fuckin' now!"

I nodded, before picking up the fight with my T-shirt again. Somehow, I managed to get it free from my back and the bed, tossing it to the side as I reached for his shorts to shove them down his hips. He yanked mine from my body -- after a brief tussle with my legs -- before covering me with his body once again.

Then he was kissing me with wicked thrusts of his tongue. He moved his hands over my body, exploring me like no man had ever touched me before.

He reached between us and his fingers found their way to my slick entrance.

He thrust one inside me, and my body arched up against him as I fought for control. But it was no use. He pushed another finger inside with a gentle, slow glide.

"Don't want to hurt you, honey. Tell me if it hurts."

"It doesn't," I whispered. "I've never had sex with a guy, but I got rid of *that* myself."

He grunted, grinding his hips against me. He removed his fingers and I felt the head of his cock at my entrance. Again, my pussy spasmed, like it was reaching for his cock, trying to pull him deep inside me. I knew that was exactly what I wanted. I thought I'd die from the pleasure, the white-hot need building in my body. I moaned in ecstasy and wrapped my arms and legs around him, wanting him even closer.

He moved in me, in and out in deep, slow strokes that drove us both to the brink of madness. His fingers dug into my hips and pulled me tight against him as if to force himself even deeper. I cried out and he lifted his head just enough to look down into my face as my orgasm overwhelmed me. I shattered around him, my pussy squeezing and pulsing around his big cock. I could feel it throbbing inside me.

Ice continued to gaze into my face as the pleasure seemed to go on and on. He gazed down at me with something like wonder. Then he let out a deep growl before he gave a loud shout and his whole body stiffened in one long, shuddering orgasm. He rocked against me and I felt him spilling his warm cum deep into my pussy. The pleasure was intense, and I let out another loud cry of my own as another wave of pleasure washed over me.

When it was over, when we both went limp and lay on the bed together, Ice kissed and nuzzled my neck gently, sweetly. Like he was praising my body's response to him. I was out of breath like I'd run a race. The feeling inside my chest said I'd won that race with gusto.

When he pulled back, I smiled up at him. He shook his head, that look of awe still on his face and I wondered if he realized his expressions were unguarded. And why was he looking at me like that?

"Ice?"

"Sweet God above, Dawn," he whispered, his voice husky and rough with his shouts of completion. "You're fuckin' perfect." He buried his face in my neck, his body slick with sweat. Was he trembling?

"Is it always like this?" My voice was small and

unsure. I knew it was but couldn't seem to stop it. I felt like I'd been stripped bare, all my faults and inexperience there for him to judge.

He barked out a laugh as he continued to kiss and lave my skin with his lips and tongue. "Honey, I've never felt anything like that in my whole life. Not with any woman I've ever had sex with. I never even imagined sex could be like that."

Despite the reminder that he'd had his pick of women he wanted, his words relaxed me. I wanted to be everything he ever needed.

"You are, honey. You fuckin' are."

"Did I say that out loud?"

His warm chuckle filled something inside me I hadn't realized was empty. "Yeah, honey. You did. And I'm glad. Because I feel the same way. I want to be everything you need, too." He framed my head with his arms, resting his weight on them as he looked down at me. "We'll be what each other needs."

"Mama said love would come later, but…"

When I didn't finish, he prodded me gently. "But what?"

"What if I thought I already loved you?"

He grinned. "What if I thought I already loved *you*?"

I smiled back up at him, placing my hand on the side of his face. "I think that sounds about perfect."

Chapter Nine

Ice

The storm got bad. Real bad. By the time I got a text from Ripper telling me it would be best to move to the inner part of the hotel, we were already heading to the ballroom with everyone else. I almost decided to stay in the bathroom and would have if it had just been me. But I wasn't risking Dawn because I didn't like to be around strange people. I could "people" sometimes, but being around strangers wasn't my thing. Probably because I was constantly looking around them trying to determine who was the biggest threat and who was the sleeper.

Dawn stayed right by my side, her hand tucked in the waistband of my jeans as we made our way to a corner of the room. I chose the innermost one. Thankfully, no one had taken it because it was on the complete opposite side from the food bar the hotel had set up.

"Stay here. I'll get us a snack and something to drink."

"OK."

Even in the crowded area, the wind howled loudly, making me nervous. There were dangers I could control and dangers I couldn't. I didn't deal with what I couldn't control. It was the reason storms made me nervous. All a person could do was hunker down until it passed.

I'd just gotten us a sandwich, chips, and a bottle of water when the lights went out. Of course, there was the collective gasp and a few screams and whimpers. It was a couple of seconds before the generator kicked on and the safety lights followed.

"It's all right, folks." Someone from the hotel

tried to calm everyone down. "We expected this. There's enough fuel for the generators for three days, and we're keeping an eye on the water. We've got plans for three meals a day and snacks for everyone here. We'll keep you as safe and comfortable as we possibly can."

I kept moving back to the corner where I'd left Dawn, snacks in hand. I had to move through several people and stopped once to help an older couple by getting them snacks. The woman was in a wheelchair and the man didn't like the idea of leaving her by herself while he got refreshments. I'd just gotten back to the snack table when my sat phone rang. Which prompted several people to check their own phones because at some point cell service and Internet had been interrupted.

"Yeah."

"Found the man you were looking for." Something in Suzie's voice clued me into the fact that something was very, very wrong.

"Whatcha got?"

"Well, let me start by saying you didn't give me much to go on. With that being said, I still got the guy."

"Give it to me."

"Before I do that -- we're still trying to track down his location -- I want to apologize for any trouble you may have in the future. I'll take full responsibility but, given your parameters, I had to go outside the box and there is a very, very, *very* slight possibility I got caught."

"Caught?" Yeah, I got a sinking feeling I knew what was coming next and I didn't know whether to laugh or cry. Now I knew how Cain felt that first time Suzie did what I thought she'd done. I didn't know whether to be proud of her or scold her.

"You gave me a name, Cliff. One. Name. That's it. And the fact that there was, and I quote, a friend who had trouble with this guy. Based on that *and* the fact that you went to find El Diablo's daughter, I went on the assumption it was her who was your friend."

"How does that relate?"

"I backtracked her from Florida back to Lexington. Cross-referenced her whereabouts with the name of your guy. David Almond. That's where I found him. Two days before Dawn left Lexington, he was at her apartment. From what I could tell, she left in a pretty bad way and headed to Louisville where she got a hotel room for the night. The next day, she left, headed to Florida."

"How'd you do all that, Suz?"

"That's the tricky part. I might have maybe kinda sorta hacked Giovanni again. But it was for a good cause!"

"Jesus. Did you at least get away clean?" Yeah. I was definitely equal parts amused and irritated.

"Well, that's the thing. This guy's a monster, Cliff. If Dawn's messed up with him, you're not safe and neither is she. When I found out about this guy, speed became more important than stealth."

"Tell me."

"There has been more than one woman go missing around him. Rumor is he killed his best friend, but they were never able to prove it. Of course, each time charges are filed against him, the prosecutor assigned gets a huge deposit. Sometimes to their personal bank in Lexington, sometimes to an offshore account. Right after, the charges are dropped."

My heart started racing. Not because I was scared of this bastard. I didn't know anything about him other than that he seemed to like beating on women. No. If I ever came face-to-face with the bastard, I'd take him out on the spot. Consequences be damned. What had me on edge was knowing that men like this didn't tolerate someone getting away from him.

"He'll be coming for her. Soon."

"That's what I'm trying to find now. Where he is in relation to you and Dawn. It's all kind of complicated, but I'm using a program -- couple of them really -- that Argent Tech scrapped as a breach of privacy. Giovanni still has it, but it's on lockdown. Took some doing to even get to it. But it tracks literally everything hooked to the net or a satellite. City cameras, cell phones, ATMs, any security system that operates on a cloud… all of it. It uses things like official ID cards, driver's licenses, and passports with facial recognition to pinpoint anyone anywhere as long as there is a positive identification on record somewhere. Me and Zora have it searching for him. If he's on any camera anywhere in the world, this program will find him."

"Good work, Suz. Keep me posted. And Suz? If Giovanni calls in a rage, apologize and swear to never do it again."

"Not sure that will work this time, Cliff. I promised that the last two times I did it."

I couldn't help but chuckle. "Yeah. You're right. How about you don't answer the phone."

"Great idea!"

Once I'd ended the call with Suzie, I headed back to Dawn. I didn't like being away from her when there was danger nearby. While we were relatively safe where we were, the storm was a big fucking danger. Every protective instinct I had was screaming at me to get back to her. Probably the combination of the storm and what I knew was a danger from Almond. Hopefully, we'd be safely on the way to the Bane compound or, better, the Bones compound before he got on her trail. Then I could form a plan of attack and not be on the defensive from the get-go. I had the upper hand simply by knowing who he was and his background and that he was coming for her.

"Everything all right?" Dawn looked up at me with a soft smile. I could tell she was nervous. Likely because of the worsening storm and us having to move from our room.

"Yes. Suzie's looking into finding Almond. Granted, she's using less than ethical means, but if she gets the job done, I could give a good Goddamn. Giovanni's gonna be pissed, but he'll get over it."

Dawn smiled. "Dad gets a kick out of hearing Suzie hacked the great Giovanni Romano. Especially since she keeps doing it no matter what he does."

"I know. I get why Cain was always equal parts amused and exasperated when she got caught. 'Course, there's been plenty of times she didn't get caught, but no one's ever pointed that out."

We passed time in silence. She ate and I kept watch over her. I kept us away from the light as much as possible. I was on edge and wasn't sure why, but one of the best things Cain had taught me was to listen to my instincts. Better to be wrong and prepared than the other way around.

I got us a couple of blankets and pillows and gave them to Dawn so she could make herself a nest to rest comfortably. She preferred to rest her head in my lap. Which, I admit, gave me all kinds of naughty ideas.

When my cock became too much to ignore,

Dawn turned her face into my lap. I sucked in a breath.

"Jesus, Dawn!" I hissed. "What're you doin'?"

"Well, if you don't know, I must not be doing it right." I couldn't see her in the dark, but the amusement in her voice was clear.

Even in the middle of a hurricane, in a public place with only a blanket to hide us, I was considering letting her play. Was it a good idea? Not in the least. But how the fuck was I supposed to turn her down when we had literally nothing else to do but wait? It was after midnight and most everyone was asleep. So when she unzipped my fly, I let my head fall back against the wall and just enjoyed.

At first, her touch was tentative. Careful. She wrapped her soft palm around my dick and stroked with a slow up-and-down motion that soon had me panting. I thought she glanced up at me a few times, but I couldn't see her clearly. Though the security lights had come on when the generators kicked in, hotel personnel had turned most of them off to conserve power and to let us rest. The lights out in the hall were still on and there were people monitoring the water but really. What were the rest of us going to do?

The moment she became comfortable, Dawn kissed the head of my cock. I couldn't help the jolt of my body. The thought of the pleasure she could give me was maddening.

Her tongue flicked against my shaft, teasing me. And, from the way she moaned softly against me, it was obvious she was enjoying herself. She took her time, flicking her tongue against the tip and wrapping her lips around my shaft as far as she could. The feeling was incredible, and soon, I wanted to tell her to take all of me in her hot little mouth. But I didn't dare. While we were a good distance away from everyone, I didn't want to draw attention. Fuck, this was tricky! I hadn't done something like this since my high school girlfriend had gone down on me in a movie theater. That had been a great adventure. This was even more thrilling.

This went on for what felt like an eternity and I could feel my body tense. My hips moved, trying to tell her without words what I needed. I was so fucking close to coming, my eyes were practically crossed.

"Dawn, pull back if you don't want this in your mouth. I'm gonna come, baby." My voice was a hoarse whisper. My hands fisted in her hair even though I'd just warned her to pull back. I'd never force her to do something she didn't want, but fuck me, I wanted to come down her throat.

Instead of pushing away, however, Dawn turned from her position on her side with her face in my lap to her belly so she could better control how deep she took me. And Goddamn if she didn't take me fucking deep.

When she had my cock as far down her throat as she could take me, she swallowed. Several times. The muscles of her throat massaged my cock until there was no fucking way I could hold back any longer.

Gritting my teeth to hold in any sound I could, I gave myself the go ahead. Cum shot out of me like a rocket down her throat. She jerked but gripped the base of my cock tighter as she continued to suck and swallow.

When I was done, I let out the breath I'd been holding. Dawn carefully peeked out from under the blanket, looking up at me. It was all I could do not to chuckle. Not because I was amused so much as I just couldn't believe she'd done this on her own.

Being part of an MC, I can't say I hadn't had sex in public with a club girl. Or two. But nothing had been as erotic as this blowjob from my inexperienced little minx. And I knew without a doubt she'd done it for me. OK, so maybe she'd wanted to experience the kink, too, but she could have gotten me to pleasure her if that had been what she'd wanted.

"I think my little angel has a definite naughty side."

"Oh? Who would that be? I'm a good girl."

I couldn't help myself this time. I chuckled as I pulled her up and across my lap so I could cuddle her close. She smelled clean and fresh. And slightly of sex. It made me want to take her back to our room and fuck her again until we both passed out.

"You're definitely a good girl. But you're also my naughty little minx."

"As long as I'm yours, I'll be whatever you want me to be."

"All you have to be is mine, Dawn. Everything else will take care of itself."

"Then I'm yours. Always."

"Always, honey."

Chapter Ten

Dawn

It was close to three in the morning. While I'd dozed in Ice's arms, I couldn't seem to fall into any kind of meaningful sleep. Not surprising given the situation.

"You awake?" Ice's whisper was next to my ear.

"Yeah. Can't sleep."

"I know. Me either. Want to get up and stretch?"

"Sure. I could use a walk. Think they'll let us go down the hall or something?"

"Yeah. We'll take a bathroom break and stretch our legs."

Quietly, we left the ballroom. There were hotel personnel in the hall milling around and keeping watch. They'd set up an area where they monitored weather radio for the area. No one paid us any attention.

The restrooms weren't far. Dawn went into the women's while I went to the men's. Seemed silly when there was no one in the area but us. I guess it was habit that had me willingly separating from her. Men didn't go into the women's restroom and vice versa.

I'd just washed my hands when my sat phone rang.

"Suz?"

"Is Dawn with you?" Uh-oh. I could tell from her tone something was really wrong.

"She's in the bathroom. What's wrong?"

"Get to her, Cliff! Get her and get out of the hotel!" That tight feeling in my gut cinched so tight I thought I might puke. Phone to my ear, I bolted from the bathroom and into the ladies' room.

"Dawn!" I wasn't quiet. "Dawn!" No answer. So

I went looking in the stalls. No one. "Mother fuck!"

I hurried out of the bathroom and into the hallway. Empty. The station the hotel had set up had only a couple of people manning it, but Dawn was nowhere I could see.

"*Dawn!*" The men at the makeshift weather center looked back at me, but Dawn was nowhere in sight.

"Talk to me, Suz! She's not here! Where the fuck is she?"

"The hotel entrance. There's an ATM next to it. She just got there. Everything else is out with the electricity. Almond is with her. He's trying to force her outside, but she's fighting him. Hurry, Cliff!"

I took off at a dead run. Thank God I'd thought to bring my gun. It was in a holster at the small of my back and I drew it now, chambering a round as I ran. Rounding the corner, I saw them. Across the darkened lobby, Dawn struggled with a man much bigger than her. She fought him, but when he backhanded her, she crumpled to the floor. Rage flooded me, making my blood boil with the need to kill this motherfucker.

Almond dragged Dawn to her feet by her hair. She cried out, her hands going to her scalp to relieve the pressure, which gave her attacker an opening to punch her abdomen. She crumpled to the floor.

"Stupid bitch! All you had to do was get me the money! If you had, I might have let you live. Now, you're going straight to hell where all bad little whores go."

I kept moving, sprinting now. The length of the lobby seemed like it was the length of a football field with me on one end and Dawn on the other.

"Get away from me!" Dawn screamed, kicking out even as she clutched the side of her belly where that bastard had kicked her. I continued to run, trying to get to her, but it felt like I was moving in quicksand. She connected with the inside of one knee and Almond screamed. So she did it again, and one more time before his knee gave way and he went down.

Dawn got to her feet and… went medieval on his ass. With a cry, she kicked and stomped before falling on him and pounding his face with her fists. Girl could throw a punch too. She didn't stay on him like that long before she got back to her feet and started kicking again. Doubtless her fists hurt, even though she'd gone for his nose instead of his cheek or other parts of his face over bone.

He fought back, managing to land a hit to her thigh just as I got to them. Dawn gave an angry scream before *stomping* the living fuck outta this guy's nuts. Where Almond had tried to fight back before, faced with a furious female fighting back, he was surprisingly passive. He tried to protect himself, but Dawn pummeled him, stomping and kicking with all the strength in her shapely legs. It didn't help that every time he tried to fight back, Dawn landed another score to his privates. I was pretty sure I heard a bone in his hand crunch more than once. The man squealed and whimpered like the little bitch he was.

"Dawn, let me take it from here."

"Motherfucker!" she screamed as she continued to pummel the guy, either not hearing or ignoring me. "Have your daddy get you out of *this*!" Another kick to his balls. "I got news for you, you son of a bitch." She kicked him again, then knelt so that she could get right in his face as she spat on him. Then she said something I didn't expect. "I was gonna have them all let you live because I didn't want to be the one to sign your death warrant. Even said so when my man finally got the truth outta me. But you know what? Neither me nor my dad will lose more of our souls by dealing with trash like you. In fact, killing you might just help him grow a piece of it back."

"Dawn." I tried to get her attention without startling her. The last thing I needed was her fighting me and this motherfucker getting away. Though, I wasn't sure the bastard was capable of doing anything other than lying there and moaning. Mostly, he just whimpered and did his best to beg her to stop. Dawn didn't take her gaze from the motherfucker currently staring up at her in confusion and horror while he cupped his groin.

"Ice, may I have your gun, please?"

"No, w-wait! Y-you c-can't do th-this! I'll b-be m-missed!" His words were muddled and he shivered in pain.

"You might be missed," Dawn conceded. "That's true. But I'm betting your family will breathe a sigh of relief they don't have to continually pay someone to keep your sorry ass out of prison, and the rest of the campus and community won't have to wonder who the next woman to be brutally raped and murdered will be." She stood before kicking him in the face this time. "Killing you will be a fucking community service."

She held out her hand like she fully expected me to just hand over my gun. To be fair, had we been somewhere safe and secluded, I might have done just that.

"You know I can't do that, honey. Not here."

The guy looked up at me, a pleading look in his eyes. "You gotta help me, man! You can see how crazy she is, right?"

"Don't know any such thing. But before I do

anything else, I need to check something."

"Check something? Are you crazy? This bitch is gonna kill me!" He was sounding stronger. Likely adrenaline giving him a little boost.

"Not if I do it first. Now my advice is for you to shut the fuck up."

I took out my sat phone and snapped a picture of the guy, sending it to Suzie before I called her.

"That the guy, Suz?"

"Oh, my God! Yes! Is Dawn OK?" Suzie sounded near tears. Figured. The woman was the most compassionate person I'd ever come across.

I started to answer that, yes, Dawn was fine, but my woman chose that moment to resume kicking Almond. How to answer Suzie?

"She will be. There's just some pent-up anger she needs to get rid of, but she seems to be doing a pretty good job of that now."

"Bastard!" As meek as Dawn had seemed these few hours I'd been with her, this was a completely new side to the woman. I'd be lying if I said it didn't turn me the fuck on. Unfortunately, I couldn't let her continue like this. We were too exposed to anyone who might walk by to let her continue her… therapy.

"Motherfucker!" She kicked him again, which was followed by another high-pitched whimper from Almond.

The wind was roaring. We were too damned close to the windows. The hotel had reinforced the windows with plywood on the outside, but the glass door had been barricaded from the inside. Almond must have removed that barrier at some point because the glass was bare. And there was debris pummeling it now.

"Dawn!" I looped an arm around her waist,

tucking my gun away as I did. Much as I wanted to shoot the guy, I couldn't. And I damned sure didn't want Dawn getting ahold of my gun. "We've got to get away from the door."

"I'm not letting this motherfucker live, Ice. He's evil!"

"I know, honey. We'll take care of him. Your father and I." I tried to lighten the mood when I had the same feelings she did about letting the bastard live. "It'll give us something to bond over so he doesn't kill me."

"He's not going to kill you." She relaxed against me but didn't take her eyes off of Almond. "He loves me too much for that. This guy, on the other hand…"

"Yeah, honey. I know." More and more debris pounded the glass of the door until something with some weight finally cracked it. "We'll kill him to death, then do it again. But we need to get the fuck away from this door. *Now*!"

I finally penetrated her rage and Dawn looked up at me, then to the door and gasped. "Yes. I'm sorry! I'm sorry!"

"Come on!" I backed us away from the door, ever mindful of the man I needed to kill but couldn't. He'd gotten to one knee but hadn't been able to rise any farther. "Don't get comfortable, you son of a bitch," I bit out. "I'll be comin' for --"

I was cut off when the door exploded inward. Dawn screamed and I turned so that my back was to the shattered door. Debris came toward us like flying shrapnel. I put my body between her and as much danger as I could despite being hit several times by small objects blown in by the storm. The wind was merciless and brutal in its intensity. We were flung forward to the ground. I landed on top of her but somehow managed to catch most of my weight so I didn't hurt her. There was no way to get us upright, so I crawled forward with Dawn underneath me until we were at the entrance to the hallway and reasonably safe.

"Ice!"

"I've got you! Stay down!" I had to yell to be heard.

Somehow, I managed to get us to the other end of the lobby and behind a wall. The wind still funneled through the building, but we were shielded enough to stand. Surprisingly, I still had the damned sat phone in my grip.

"Stay here." I gave her a hard kiss before holding her gaze to make sure she did what I told her. When she nodded, I handed her the phone, which was still on the open call to Suzie, then I pulled my gun and moved back toward the lobby. I had to make sure I didn't lose David Almond.

Emergency lights gave me some visual cues throughout the room, including Almond kneeling by the door where we'd left him. A metal rod protruded from his chest. He looked stunned as he wrapped his fingers around the rod. As I watched, a piece of concrete from the barrier wall isolating the check-in canopy tore through the door and smashed into him, exploding his head on impact.

"Good fuckin' riddance."

I hurried over to Dawn just as hotel security charged into the lobby.

"Holy shit! What happened?"

"He should have stayed away from the fuckin' door is what happened."

"Did you shoot him?" The guard pointed at the gun I'd drawn.

"Well, I didn't play fuckin' patty-cake with the bastard," I muttered.

"What?" The noise from the wind was horrible. Carrying on a conversation was impossible. Instead of trying, I pointed to the slab of concrete before turning back to Dawn. Fuck the ballroom, I was taking her back to our room. We'd manage or we wouldn't. But I wasn't taking her where she had to be around people after this ordeal. I still didn't know exactly what happened and I needed to make sure she was all right.

"Where are you going?" One of the security guys followed us.

"I'm taking my woman back to our room. She needs to get dry and I need to make sure she wasn't hurt."

"What about that dead guy?"

I stopped, turning to face him. "My advice is to go back to the command center you guys set up outside the ballroom for storm updates. Ignore everything else. The people in that shelter need you there worse than that guy."

The guy nodded, swallowing. He was pale and didn't look like he was up for trying to store a dead body. Hopefully, they'd all wait the storm out and let emergency services take care of it later. While I was glad I didn't have to get Thorn involved in my mess, I was oddly dissatisfied with the way the guy had died. I'd wanted to do it myself.

When I reached her, Dawn held up her arms to me and I lifted her, carrying her down the hall. She clung to me, sobbing into my neck, which tore at my heart. I was responsible for keeping her safe. I'd promised I would and she'd almost been taken by some kind of sociopath right under my fucking nose.

It took little time to get back to our room. Once

there, I set her in the bathroom. "Stay here. I'll be right back with some pillows and blankets. OK?"

"Please hurry, Ice. I don't want to be alone." She was trembling and soaked to the skin. No doubt the adrenaline had worn off, leaving her feeling like shit.

I grabbed enough bedding to make us comfortable for a while, along with one of my large shirts, then joined her in the bathroom and shut the door. She'd turned on the flashlight on her phone so I could see while I set the couch cushions and pillows on the floor before spreading out a couple of sheets and blankets from the bed, so we could rest and hold each other until the storm lessened.

We settled there on the floor. I had my back to the wall while Dawn sat sideways in my lap, clinging to me like I was her lifeline. I knew she was mine.

"I could have fuckin' lost you, honey."

"I'm OK. I'm here and I'm fine. He's dead."

"Yeah. He is." I was sure I was trembling as hard as she was. "He's fuckin' dead, but he died too easy. What happened? How'd he get you?"

"He followed me in after you went inside the men's bathroom. He knew my family had money and said he needed more than what he'd already stolen from me."

"Did he say why?"

"I know the answer to that!" The voice came faintly from the phone still clutched in Dawn's hand. I barked out a laugh.

"You didn't drop the phone."

Dawn blinked up at me in confusion, then gasped. She held the phone up. "I didn't even realize I still had it. Oh, my God!"

I took it from her and put it on speaker. "Suzie?"

"Yes. I stayed on when I realized you guys were

in danger. I needed to know what happened so I could tell the guys. They're on the way to get you, by the way."

"Who is?"

"Thorn's men. I'm sorry, Cliff, but I couldn't get you to talk to me and I wasn't leaving you there alone."

I chuckled, knowing my sister would come through for us, no matter that I'd told her to not say anything to anyone other than Zora. "I owe you big time, Suz."

"Just get home safely."

"What'd you find? You said you knew why Almond needed money?"

"Yes. Apparently, he used a bunch of drugs he was supposed to sell. Now the supplier wants his money. I didn't have time to get much but suffice it to say his life was in danger. He thought his father could buy him out of this, but apparently, his parents had reached their limit. Probably had something to do with the last rape and murder he was suspected of. They couldn't keep it quiet because the girl's father was a former state legislator."

"He was a monster. I'd say he was a psychopath. He lured women to him, pretending to care, then…"

"Yeah." Dawn shivered and cuddled more securely into me. "Though I don't really think he had his family fooled. They simply didn't care."

"At least," Suzie added, "not until he killed a woman who was somebody. Someone they considered in their class."

"Sounds to me like they all deserve each other." I rested my chin on top of Dawn's head and rubbed back and forth over her silky hair, holding her as tightly as she held me.

"You guys good?" Suzie sounded equal parts relieved and nervous. I knew my sister well enough to know she wouldn't rest easy until this storm moved on.

"I think so. I've got us shut in the bathroom with some cushions and blankets. I think we'll be good here for a while. Probably shoulda just stayed here in the first Goddamned place."

"No. You did what you should have done. No one could have known that bastard was already there."

"How'd he find her anyway?"

"He followed her. If you hadn't found her when you did, he'd have her. He wasn't that far behind her. Thankfully, she always stopped at very crowded gas stations or he'd have snatched her on the way to Florida. I'm sorry it took me so long to find him. If I'd been quicker --"

"Stop it, Suzie. I absolutely won't have you thinking you could have done anything more. You did exactly what I asked you to do. If it hadn't been for you, I might have been too late."

"If everyone's good now, I'm going to end the call." That was Cain.

"Dad?"

"Yeah, Ice. Your dad. And the man who pays the fuckin' company sat phone bill."

"Dad! Cliff and Dawn almost died! Who cares about the phone bill!" I could hear Suzie's outrage, but I also knew my dad. He was just as worried as Suzie, if not more.

I chuckled. It was my father's way of dealing. His gruff and grouchy side came out in spades. "We're fine. And he's right, Suz. We need to save the battery and the minutes."

"Had a call from El Diablo."

I had to suppress the groan. "Of course, you did. And I'm totally calling him a tattletale." As I'd hoped, that got a giggle from Dawn. Good.

"Yeah? Let me know how that works out for you."

"If he told you to talk me into letting Dawn go, that's between me and her. If, after this, she doesn't want me, I'll let her go back to her home. But no one, not even El Diablo, the bad-ass assassin, is going to take her from me if she doesn't want to go."

"You really feel that much for his daughter?"

"I do, Cain. She's my one."

"Then there shouldn't be any problem. You just need to convince her daddy."

I snorted. "Right."

"My dad isn't the boogeyman, you know." Dawn looked up at me and smiled.

"Yeah?" I could almost see Dad's raised eyebrow. "Tell that to… well, everyone who's not you, your siblings, or your mother." He chuckled. "Be safe, son. Your mom says she loves you."

"I love her too."

"I'm proud of you, Ice." Then he ended the call.

Chapter Eleven

Dawn

The storm lasted just over twenty-four hours before it finally passed. There was water *everywhere*. Thankfully, our hotel managed to make it through without more damage, and Ice and me got to stay in the bathroom and cuddle. And fuck. Just a little.

Hotel security called EMS to come get David's body. Surprisingly, no one asked me or Ice what had happened. Ice had shrugged and said it was pretty obvious what had happened. I got the feeling words had been exchanged somewhere to ease that path, but I wasn't asking too many questions.

It took us a while to get out of town and back on the road to Lake Worth. Mainly because Ice's truck had a big-ass tree through the windshield. Salvation's Bane came through for us big time, though. They were there even before we left the hotel and stepped into the parking lot.

Red and Grease from Bane hefted the tree out and got the truck running. They offered the truck they'd brought and Ice was going to take me back to Black Reign, but that didn't feel right. So I talked him into staying. He and his brothers from his sister club fixed everything together. Then they worked on the other cars in the parking lot. And the hotel door.

This was why I loved being part of a club. Sure, Salvation's Bane wasn't a traditional MC. My dad was fucking loaded. He put all kinds of money into it that most MCs didn't have, but he always made sure he gave back to the community. They all did. It was why he had me. It's how he and my mom had found me. They took me in and gave me a home and love, and I knew I never wanted to be away from that kind of family ever again.

I smiled as we pulled onto the road leading to the Black Reign compound. Reaching over, I squeezed Ice's knee. He winked at me.

"You good, honey?"

"I can honestly say I don't think I've been better in my life." I knew the smile on my face stretched from ear to ear. I couldn't remember a time when I was as happy as I was right now.

The distant rumble of motorcycles came to me faintly on the breeze where the windows were down. OK, so they weren't exactly down because of choice. They were broken and Red had removed the rest of the glass so I didn't get injured. He and Grease had followed us, but it wasn't Red's bike or the truck and trailer Grease had been driving I was hearing.

As we made it to the gate, I saw a couple motorcycles fall into line behind us. Then a few more. By the time we got to the compound, there were a couple of dozen bikers, some with old ladies behind them, proudly rolling in with us.

"Oh, my God! How many bikers did you bring with you, Ice?"

"No one. Red and Grease did it on their own. Not sure where everyone else came from..." He trailed off before a huge grin split his face. "My brothers."

"From Bane?"

"Yeah." He glanced at me, that grin turning into a smile of contented satisfaction. "And Bones."

"They came all this way? Why?"

"Dunno. Guess we'll find out shortly."

We pulled into the parking lot, and Ice tugged me until I slid across the seat and out his side with him. Bikes pulled up all around us as the men riding them revved their motors. Black Reign members filed out of the main clubhouse to greet everyone with claps on the back and bro hugs.

"Hey there, prez." Daniel -- Cyclone -- gave his brother a firm handshake. "Thought we'd come see how the two of you were settling in."

"Word got around fast, huh." Ice shook his head, rolling his eyes even as he smiled.

"Well, once Suzie found out what you were up against, I got the guys together and headed this way. Thorn sent a contingent as well just to piss off El Diablo."

"Why do I get the feeling you're not talking about that fucker Almond." Ice narrowed his eyes at Cyclone.

"That scrawny runt? Hell, no. If you couldn't deal with the likes of him, you don't need to be president of Bones. No. We knew you had him covered." The man grinned. "I was talking about El Diablo."

"What?" I gasped. "You all came here to support Ice against my father?"

"Well, sweetheart, he's a pretty big deal. You know. The most prolific assassin in, you know, the *world*."

"My dad loves me." I felt the need to defend my father even though I got what they meant. "He only wants me to be happy. And Ice makes me happy."

"After less than forty-eight hours? Yeah. He's gonna question that."

Several more big men with their women approached us, smiles on their faces. The women introduced themselves to me with hugs and smiles while the men congratulated Ice with claps on the back and shoulder that looked like they'd leave bruises. My adoptive sister was one of them.

"I've missed you, girl!" Magenta gave me a tight hug. "Dad's gonna flip and it's gonna be fun to watch." She smiled brightly as she pulled back. "Sword said he'd been looking forward to this for a long time. Apparently, he thinks having El Diablo's attention on Ice means he'll back off him."

"Right." There was no way to keep from chuckling. "As long as he's been together with you, as long as he's known El Diablo, you'd think he'd have learned our dad better than that."

"I know, right?"

I have no idea who stayed at the Bones compound, but the group showed up in force. Even Stunner was there, though without Suzie or their young daughter. The man looked like he was ready to do battle. Which is to say, scary as fuck.

"You ready, honey?" Ice smiled down at me.

"Ready for what?"

"You know. To go talk to your dad. We'll have to do that before you pack up to move back to Kentucky."

I stared at him for a full minute, letting the moment linger because it was too fucking funny not to.

"You're scared of my father. Aren't you?" I grinned.

"I am not!" He frowned, narrowing his eyes at me.

"You totally are." I laughed as I wrapped my arms around his middle. "Don't worry, big guy. I'll protect you."

"Like bloody hell." He grumbled but held me close before kissing the top of my head and turning us toward the clubhouse. "Let's go. We need to get back to the Bane compound so we can help them with the clean-up."

We didn't even make it into the clubhouse before

my father and his two closest men met us outside in the entryway. El Segador leaned against the doorframe with his arms crossed. His woman, Swan, stood next to him, a huge smile on her face. Rycks and Lyric were on the other side. El Diablo was scowling at Ice as we approached. Yeah. My dad liked to be dramatic from time to time. Good thing my mother was there to mellow him out.

Mom pushed past my dad and hurried to me. "Oh, baby! I was so worried!" She pulled me into her arms, moving slightly to one side. "Let me look at you. Did you get hurt?"

"No, Mom. Ice took wonderful care of me." Her gaze slid to Ice before going back to me.

"Are you sure about him, sweetheart?" She whispered her question, so it was for our ears only. "Because if he took advantage of you…"

"No, Mom. Ice would never do that. He saved me when I thought I was going to drown, then kept me safe. When David came after me, Ice was hot on his heels. He got me away from him and kept me safe."

"It's been less than two days, sweetie. Maybe you guys can see each other over the next few months and go from there." She smiled to take the sting out of her words, but she was slowly but steadily separating me from Ice. So I planted my feet and refused to take another step.

"You're not getting me away from him, Mom. Ice is my choice." I looked over her shoulder to find Ice. My dad was in his face, looking as furious as I'd ever seen him. "I can't believe you helped him, Mom." I tried not to feel betrayed but honestly. If anyone should understand my feelings, it was my mother. After all, she'd married my dad when he'd basically forced her from her home. It didn't matter that she'd been a prisoner there. She hadn't really wanted to leave, preferring the devil she knew to the devil she didn't.

"We just want what's best for you, sweetheart."

"Ice is what's best for me." I made my voice firm, trying to imitate the tone I'd heard my mother use more than once when standing up to my father. "I might not have dated much, but I know what I want. Besides, you'll never be able to find a man better able to protect me. He's not only a soldier, but he's got an entire club of soldiers to protect all their women. He's basically got his own private army at his disposal if he needs it." I pointed to my father. "Wasn't that the whole reason Dad first set his sights on Bones? Before he took over Black Reign?"

My mother turned slightly to catch my father's gaze. My father was currently staring down Ice, but I knew he heard every word I'd said. "She's got you there, honey. I got nothin' else."

Dad rolled his eyes and gave my mother an irritated look. "Well, try harder."

"Nope. You don't want this match, that's on you. It's what Dawn wants. Far as I'm concerned, she's old enough to decide what man she wants."

"He's too old for her," Dad snapped. "She's nineteen and he's in his thirties!"

"I know you didn't just say that." Mom frowned and put her hands on her hips. "Pretty sure there's a bigger age gap between you and me than there is between Ice and Dawn."

Ice looked ready to fight but made no move to actually attack. Which was good. Though, it wasn't lost on me or anyone else in Black Reign that the whole of Bones and Salvation's Bane had lined up behind Ice to have his back.

"Liam, take a look around you." Mom was the only one who ever called my dad by his real name. It was how Dad knew he needed to step back and pay attention to her when he wouldn't for anyone else. "Two clubs have Ice's back. Not necessarily to fight you, but to help Ice keep his woman. She'll be protected. If Ice can't love her like she needs, she knows how to get home. You can always kill him later, but you can't bring him back."

"Gee, thanks, Mom." I hurried to Ice so I could stand between him and my dad. "Back off, Dad."

"Sweet girl, he's not right for you. Besides, I owe him one for threatening to take you away from home."

"You lay a finger on him and I'll hurt you worse." I bared my teeth at my father. I'd never challenged him before and I didn't do it lightly now. I had too much respect for him. But sometimes, the only language he understood was force. While I would never get physical with him, I knew I had to stand up for what I wanted. Otherwise, I wouldn't be allowed to date until I was at least thirty. Maybe forty.

As I knew it would, that got my dad's attention. What I wasn't expecting was the huge smile on his face. "Well. I guess that's all I need to know about that." He held his hand out to Ice. "Welcome to the family. *Son*."

Cyclone burst out laughing while Sword had a big ol' shit-eating grin on his face.

"Thank God," Sword chuckled. "It'll be good to have some company."

Dad pointed at the big man. "You're still in the doghouse, you know."

"Come on! Cylone and Magenta both forgave me for attacking Chloe when I first met her. So did Foster." Foster was Sword's eldest son. He'd witnessed Sword's outburst when Chloe had come to Bones. He was in his late teens now but had always been fiercely protective of his mother. When he'd seen how upset Magenta had been, the boy had refused to let Sword in the house until he made things right with Magenta. Magenta had refused to forgive Sword until Chloe forgave him. It had been a tense few weeks for Sword's family. Now, though, Sword had embraced his eldest daughter, the daughter he hadn't known he had, and Chloe seemed to adore him just as much.

"Doesn't mean they should have."

"Dad, you're always looking for reasons not to like Sword. Just as he's probably doing the same. It's time you back off and let us live our lives."

"Now, Dawn. I have no problem with you girls living your lives. I just happen to think the men you chose could be better."

I stuck my chin up, poking my dad in the chest with my finger. "You saying you didn't teach me good judgment?"

"Of course, I did. But your heart isn't something I can teach."

I stared at my father for a long time, trying to read in his face what was going on in his head. Then I saw it. The smallest gleam in his eyes.

"You asshole!" I shoved at his chest. "You don't think Ice isn't good enough for me. You're *happy* I'm with him! Why are you pretending otherwise?" I turned to my mother. "Not cool, Mom!"

"Now, now, my dear. You can't expect an old man to not protest when he has to put his beloved daughter in the hands of another man. But your Ice there knows the score. He knows who I am and that I won't hesitate to kill him if he does wrong by you." When he said that last part, he gave Ice a hard look. "I also happen to know he's a good man. I've watched him grow up and Cain is a trusted ally."

Ice grinned, not in the least perturbed. "She'll be my world." His smile broadened into a huge smile. "Daddy."

El Segador barked out a laugh and Samson snorted.

"Think you might have met your match in that young pup, El Diablo." Rycks was all kinds of amused, as was everyone else if the smothered chuckles were anything to go by.

"Indeed." Dad clapped Ice on the shoulder. "Come, everyone! Let's celebrate! Tomorrow, we'll band together to help in the clean-up."

Everyone shouted their approval and moved inside. Turned out, my father had prepared a feast. He'd approved of the match all along. Ice had told me about his conversation with my father before, and I had no doubt Dad had needed to have time to adjust to the idea of me being with Ice. Once he'd processed, he'd realized Ice would be a good match. Not only was Ice part of a club my father approved of, Ice was now president. A powerful man.

Dad pulled me into his arms and hugged me fiercely. "Ice is a good man. He will protect you as ruthlessly as I ever could."

"You have a funny way of showing your trust." I sighed, but I had a smile on my face.

"I had to make sure he wouldn't cave to anyone regarding you. Even me."

My mother was beside us, pulling me away from Dad and into her arms. "I'm sorry, sweetheart. You know your father loves to test people. This time, I agreed with him."

Ice took me from my parents, pulling me into his

arms and kissing the top of my head. "No hard feelings," he said. "Dawn is worth any interrogation or test you can throw at me. I'll figure out a way to pass and keep her."

"Good." Dad gestured to the clubhouse. "Let's celebrate."

Epilogue

Ice

The next few days were filled with work, work, and more work. I loved every second of it. I took that time to get to know Dawn better and found she was a force to be reckoned with. She was equal parts her mother and father with interesting, beautiful bits of her own unique personality thrown in for good measure. While her mother ran the clubhouse -- where they prepared food and a place to crash for many of the homeless and displaced people in the community -- Dawn ran the mobile distribution trucks while they handed out water and non-perishable items. To say I was proud was a vast understatement.

When it was finally time to head back to Kentucky, Dawn was as exhausted as I was. But it was a great tired. I'd helped people who needed it, and my woman had been by my side the whole time. Yeah. We were going to be an unstoppable team.

We rolled into the Bones compound and Suzie rushed out to greet us.

"Cliff!" When I got out of the truck, Suzie threw herself into my arms. "I'm so glad you and Dawn are OK. I was terrified when you couldn't find her!" She quickly moved on to Dawn, giving my woman a beautiful, welcoming smile. "I'm so glad Ice found you, Dawn. You'll be my sister now."

"I'll be proud to be your sister, Suzie. I heard what you did. Has Giovanni started bitching yet?"

Suzie giggled. "If he has, he's not bitched to me. I think he's kind of resigned himself. He'll never be able to keep me out!"

Everyone in the club who hadn't come to Palm Beach welcomed me and Dawn back. The club girls kept to themselves, knowing this was a family night. I wasn't worried about them, though. After seeing the way Dawn fought off her nightmare, I had no doubt she could handle herself with a few overly aggressive club girls.

"Ice?" Dawn wrapped her arms around my waist as she looked up at me.

"Yeah, honey." I smiled down at her and brushed a lock of hair off her forehead and tucked it behind her ear.

"Take me to bed."

"Now, that's the best idea I've heard all day."

That night, I made love to my woman. Several times. She even woke me with her mouth around my cock. That had ended with her on her hands and knees while I railed her from behind. My beautiful woman loved every second of it. As evidenced by the fact that she demanded I do it again.

"You're settling in nicely." Cain visited me regularly. I often bounced ideas off him or asked for advice, but I tried to work my way through most things on my own.

"It's been a surprisingly smooth transition. Helped that most of the men already respected me. I have you to thank for that. You never cut me slack."

Cain waved me off. "You and Daniel were eager to learn. I simply nurtured that part and taught you everything I could. It was your hard work that made the difference."

"How are Bohannon and Torpedo doing in Nashville?"

"They've decided the easiest thing to do is to take over Kiss of Death. It was same as decimated, but they've found a few good men to help them take it over." He shrugged. "Shouldn't be hard. The whole place has been in chaos since we took down the club hierarchy. They took over The Dark in Nashville. Bane burned down the one in Palm Beach, but they had another one in Nashville that was just as bad. That's where Torpedo says he'll start. Having a BDSM club in town is great, but he's making it into a safe place for people in that lifestyle to play. Also, it'll be a good place to launder money if we need to."

"Good. Tell them if they need anything, they're welcome to whatever resources I can send their way."

"I'll pass it on. How's your lovely woman?"

I couldn't help but smile. "She's perfect. Gave her my property patch and I don't think she's taken it off voluntarily even once. I have to make her take it off when we go to bed." I chuckled. "Never thought I'd have a woman so proud to be with me."

Cain chuckled. "She's a fine old lady, Ice. You keep her happy."

"No worries there. I'll move heaven and earth if I have to."

Dawn chose that moment to pop her head in my office. "Hi, Cain." She gave my dad a little wave. "Can I borrow Ice for a little bit?"

"Absolutely, you can." Cain stood and gave Dawn a hug. "You take care of him, young lady. He needs looking after."

"I promise. I love him."

"He loves you too." He cleared his throat before throwing up a hand at me. "Call your mother." That was his way of telling me he wanted to hear from me too.

"Every Sunday and Wednesday, Dad."

Cain grunted and headed out of my office. I turned my attention to Dawn.

"Now. What is so important you had to interrupt

my meeting with Cain. Hmm?"

She gave me a brilliant smile. "I'm horny."

I couldn't help it. I belly laughed, swinging Dawn up into my arms and heading for our rooms on the third floor of the massive clubhouse building.

"We'll have to see what we can do about that."

"See that you do. It's a very serious condition."

"I have no doubt."

Inside our home, the door locked, my woman naked in my arms, I made love to Dawn. She was always a giving, responsive lover and today was no different. After we'd both come and we lay spent in our bed, I reached to the nightstand and pulled out a small box.

"I've been waiting to give you this. Thought I'd give it a few months so we could both be sure, but I can't. I mean, what's the point? You're already wearing my property patch and I already can't ever imagine my life without you."

I handed her the velvet box and held my breath while she looked from the tiny cube to me and back again. "What is it?"

I chuckled. "Open it and see."

With trembling fingers, she did. Then she gasped, pulling the diamond solitaire from the box and sliding it on her finger.

"Oh, Ice. It's so beautiful!"

"Not nearly as beautiful as you, honey."

She rolled over so that she lay on top of me. My cock poked her entrance and she eagerly accepted me. Dawn kissed me with slow, languid strokes of her lips and tongue.

"I love you, Ice. I'll always love you."

"I love you too, honey."

She rode me. Slowly at first, then with more

vigor until she threw back her head with a sharp cry. Her pussy milking my cock triggered my own orgasm and I emptied myself inside her, grunting as I did.

Dawn stayed on top of me, my cock still buried in her hot, tight pussy. I thought she'd gone to sleep.

"Ice?"

"Yeah, baby."

"Thanks for coming for me."

"I'll always come for you, Dawn. You're my woman."

"I know. But I wasn't then, and you could have let Thorn handle it. I'm glad you didn't."

"Me too, honey. More than I can ever express."

My life was one series of fortunate events after another. Cyclone was my brother, but luck led me to Suzie. Stunner had kept us all safe and sent us to Bones. Bones had protected us and given us Cain and Angel to raise, protect, and guide us. And a hurricane had led me to Florida where I'd found Dawn. The rest was up to me and I fully intended to never take for granted all life had given me.

I was truly blessed.

And I was thankful.

Cyclone (Bones MC 15)
A Bones MC Romance
Marteeka Karland

Cyclone -- I might be a whirlwind when I get angry or hyper-focused on something, but I'm usually the laid-back brother. I'm calm, cool, and collected under fire. Until I'm not. My passions burn hot but cool quickly, and any woman in my bed knows that. Which is why I make a point to only take women who know the score. I'm up for a good time, but that's it. My club comes first. I don't have time for, nor do I want, a permanent woman. Then a party happens and I make a huge mistake. When I finally come to my senses, I realize this is one mistake that could cost me my position as vice president of Bones MC. And my life.

Willa -- To say my daddy is a shade over-protective is the understatement of the century. I try to be a good girl -- and really, I'm sure the car in the tree was *not* my fault -- but trouble seems to find me and hold me hostage. Sneaking into a Bones MC party, though? That was all me. I was lonely. And bored. I called it an early Christmas present to myself. Unfortunately, when I was downing Long Island Ice Teas, I didn't take into account that I'd never drunk alcohol before. Next thing I know I wake up in bed with one of the men from the club. I have no idea what we did or if I enjoyed myself, but I'm pleasantly sore, and there are condom wrappers all over the place. Then my gaze collides with the man who's draped half over me. Yeah. This isn't going to end well.

Chapter One

Cyclone

"Hey there, baby. How about I take you on tonight for a good time?" A svelte brunette with big tits straddled my lap in a bid for my attention. I was pretty sure I'd had her a few times but wasn't certain. Especially not now. I was drunk off my fucking *ass*. And getting drunker by the moment.

"Another time, sugar." Right. Not any time soon. I didn't keep coming back to the same women. Not often. And not without some time between fucks. The last thing I needed at this point was a woman clinging to me.

"Come on, Cyclone." The woman's whiny voice was getting on my everloving last nerve. "You've not been with any of us in weeks. It's my turn." She pouted, her plump red lips begging to be kissed. If I hadn't already told her no, I might have given in. I'd learned a long time ago not to give the club whores a reason to go against me. If I did, she'd be pushing back every inch she could. Reversing myself with her was the best reason she could have.

"I said no," I growled at her, pushing up from my chair. The room spun, but I refused to give into it, concentrating on keeping a steady gait. Moving toward the bar, I signaled the prospect behind the bar for a beer. It was probably time to slow down on the hard liquor. The younger man nodded once and pulled out a Bud Light from the fridge. He handed me the bottle unopened because everyone knew I was picky about shit like that.

"Thanks." I gave the prospect a nod before moving away from the bar to a table with a few of my other brothers. Most of them had a woman either on their lap or kneeling in front of them, giving them head.

As party clubs went, Bones had pretty mild parties. But occasionally, the guys needed to let off some steam. Tonight was one of those nights. Normally my brother, Ice, would be here with me. He kept the demons at bay for me. Ice had a woman now. Dawn was the daughter of El Diablo from Black Reign in Lake Worth, Florida. While I was happy for my brother, that made me the most eligible bachelor in the fucking club. Which meant the club girls were getting more aggressive.

Not interested.

The second I sat down, one of the girls near me turned and straddled my hips. "Been lookin' for you all night, baby." She ground herself over my crotch. While I was at half mast, I wasn't really feeling it. Likely the alcohol. Besides, the bitch had so much perfume on I could barely breathe.

I lifted her by the waist and set her on the floor. "Not tonight." I turned her away from me. "Go find someone else."

She looked back over her shoulder, pouting prettily. It was all I could do to keep from rolling my eyes. Being the president's son had gotten me women since I was old enough to not look like a fresh-faced kid. But that attention was nothing compared to what I got the second I became vice president. Now all of a sudden I literally had to throw women out of my room every fucking night. I was going to have to take some kind of stand before I lost my temper.

This woman just wouldn't take the fucking hint. Instead of slinking away to find another brother to bother, she climbed right back on my lap, this time fusing her lips against mine. When she thrust her tongue into my mouth, I thought I might puke. And not just because of the alcohol. I think the woman had gargled with curry and onions.

I grabbed her upper arms and shoved her off me before using the neckline of my T-shirt to scrub my mouth. "Christ! Wha' the fuck'd you eat?" My words were slurring but I didn't care. The fucking *taste*! "You swaller a fuckin' skunk?"

"What the fuck, Cyclone?" the woman screeched. I winced at the sound. It was about as pleasing as nails on a chalkboard and had my fucking head throbbing. "All you had to do was say you weren't interested."

"Pretty sure I already told you to find someone else." The hit of adrenaline I got from trying to fight off the nausea cleared my head somewhat, but I still wasn't in any way sober. Not even a little.

"You said you wanted me. I was gonna be your old lady, Dan."

"Never in hell have I *ever* been that drunk. I don't think it's even possible to be that drunk." I stood, somehow managing to be steady on my feet. When I took a step toward her, she wisely backed up. "Ain't never hurt a woman who didn't need it, but the only name you're allowed to call me is Cyclone. Get me?" I stared her down. Hard. The woman backed up several steps before tripping over her high-heeled boots and falling on her ass. A couple of the nearby club girls giggled or outright laughed at the busty blonde as she fumed. "You ain't ever gonna be my old lady. Only an old lady gets to call me by my given name." I pointed a finger at her. "You ever call me by anything other than my road name again... I'll fuckin' kill you."

The common room was quiet except for the music. Thankfully, the brothers had it at a reasonable level. It was better for my head but did nothing to suppress my explosion. Everyone was a witness. While I hated to be a spectacle -- didn't seem very vice presidential -- perhaps it was better this way. The club girls were getting far too aggressive, all of them either trying to land me or worm their way between my brother, Ice, and his new woman. A couple of the newer ones had even tried for Stunner. I only thought Stunner was vicious. Suzie, though...

I remember how he'd beat the shit out of one of the prospects in Bones -- Pig -- when said prospect had harassed Suzie. She'd been just a kid at the time. The beating had been epic. My father had taken his own turn too, but Stunner was the one Pig still remembered to this day. Apparently Stunner had taught his wife a few tricks in that department because Suzie had turned into a real badass over the years.

OK, so not really. But no one messed with her man. She was just as possessive as Stunner was. Which made me smile. Until I realized everyone was looking at me like I'd lost my mind. Probably because I'd gone from furious to grinning. Yeah. Likely thought I was crazy.

"Fuck this shit." I slammed my bottle down on the table next to me and stomped off. Last thing I needed to do was to lose my temper worse than I already had. I wasn't a really good drunk.

I managed to make it outside before I sank into a chair. The weather was cool but still warmer than usual for this late in the year. What little bite there was, I welcomed. With my anger evaporating, so was my clarity. Yeah. I'd drunk way more than I should have.

Looking up at the night sky, I took a deep breath. Stars twinkled overhead in the darkness. Gradually I closed my eyes and just let my head spin. There wasn't anything I could do other than not drink any more and maybe sleep it off. The cool air was soothing, easing the nausea that had threatened earlier from the overabundance of perfume.

I had nearly dozed off when someone stumbled into me. There was a sharp, feminine cry, then a small figure fell into my lap. Literally.

She giggled. "I'm so sorry." Her apology was ruined when she giggled again. "I really am sorry, but falling is just so funny." The woman's laughter was musical. And familiar, though I couldn't place where I'd heard it. When she sighed and rubbed her face in the crook of my neck like she belonged there, I didn't really care.

I knew I should probably tell her to get the hell away from me, but for some stupid reason, my arms closed around the small figure. She either didn't notice or didn't care because she never moved her face from my neck. She *did* inhale. Deeply.

"God, you smell good…"

"You too, sugar." Too late I realized I'd voiced my musings out loud, but I wasn't about to take it back. The woman smelled like heaven. Like lavender and spring rain. Her lips were soft against my skin, driving me crazy, when I didn't welcome the sensation. I didn't *need* a woman. I never wanted anyone to have any power over me. But this woman could make me reevaluate that position.

This wasn't a club girl. She didn't smell right. All the women here tried to outdo themselves in the perfume department most of the time. No. This girl was fresh and sweet. It was dark outside, and I couldn't see her clearly, but I was sure she didn't belong at this party. Though her form was slight but curvy in all the right places, she didn't have the feel of the women here. Unless she was new, but I'd have known if she were. Anyone coming to the club had to be approved by Ice, me, or Stunner. We liked knowing who was in our midst.

"Mmmmm…" She latched on to my neck with her mouth, sucking and quite possibly leaving her mark. Strangely, I found my hand going to her head to hold her there, encouraging her to continue when I should really push her away.

But, God, her gentle sucking and licking felt good! It was her scent combined with the tentative way she touched. Other than her mouth on my skin, she didn't do more than rest one palm against my chest. The other was pinned between her body and mine.

"Like my taste?" My voice was rough and slightly slurred, but I couldn't be bothered to care all that much.

"Um-hmm…" She sounded so contented it made me feel like I'd accomplished something truly incredible. Given my drunken state, maybe I had and didn't remember it. "You taste like heaven." Her breathy whisper made my already interested cock swell in anticipation. "Could lick you all night long."

She sucked at my neck again, the little sting making me groan. Wasn't I annoyed before when that club girl had blanketed me with her body? I had no idea who the other woman was, but this woman… yeah. Whole world of difference. Though, I had no idea who she was. I mean, there was something familiar about her. I just couldn't place what.

"You're welcome to lick me as long as you want." I bunched my hand in her hair. Where before I held her gently, now I wanted to control her movements. Needed to control the woman. Still, that nagging feeling I knew her, and that I probably shouldn't be doing this kept me in check. Somewhat.

At least, I didn't just take what I wanted when it was so freely offered.

She shifted so that she straddled me much like the club girl had. They'd been on me every day since the day I became vice president. This girl was different. I couldn't put my finger on it, but despite her actions, there was a vibe of innocence about her. Yet another reason I needed to stop this madness.

But, Goddamn, it felt fucking good!

No. Not "it." The woman. It was her touch that felt good. Her kisses. Her scent. All of it. Everything about what was happening.

Somehow, she brushed her lips against mine. It wasn't a bold kiss. Rather, it was tentative. Like she was experimenting.

"Mmmm…" She hummed in pleasure as she continued to brush her mouth over mine. I opened my mouth and darted my tongue out to lick at the seam of her lips. She gasped in a breath and stilled. So I did it again. This time, she moaned, her body trembling in my arms.

I pulled back to gaze into her eyes. In the dim light, I could see little of her face, but her eyes were a sparkling blue. The crescent moon was reflected in the glittering depths, and I saw arousal shining back at me.

"You want me, sugar?"

She shuddered, whimpering. "I do. Please."

With a grunt, I stood, the woman securely in my arms. She wrapped her legs around my waist and hung on as I stalked back into the clubhouse, just wishing a motherfucker would say something. As much as I wanted this woman, I wasn't fucking her out in the open. For one thing, it might be warmish outside, but it was still December in Kentucky. Getting her naked was going to happen, but it would happen inside the clubhouse. In private.

Normally, I'd take her to an empty room, or, if she was a club girl, I'd go to her room. But I didn't know if she had quarters here or where she was staying. Besides, I wanted her in my room. Why? Beat the fuck outta me. But there was something driving me that way. Call it blind instinct. I was taking this woman to my room. To my bed. And, if I had my way, I wasn't letting her out until we were both well and truly satisfied.

Assuming I managed to get there without falling on my face. Perhaps I should have stuck to beer tonight. The Jack Daniels was hitting me harder than it should have. Or maybe I'd just drunk that much. Thank God I didn't have whiskey dick because there was no way I was willingly missing the chance to fuck this woman.

* * *

Willa

God, had a man ever smelled this good? There was an underlying hint of gasoline all the men in Bones had, but there was something woodsy and wild about this man. Fresh-cut hay and cedar mixed with a feral scent that drew me in like a bee to honey. It was too dark to really tell who had me and I didn't really care. Especially when he made me feel this good.

I'd been heading back inside the clubhouse when I'd fallen into his lap. Literally. His voice was familiar, though I'd never heard the husky drawl the way he spoke to me while I was in his arms.

My head spun and I felt like I was flying. Though I'd been buzzing pretty hard before I ended up in the arms of this man, I was pretty sure the last three shots of Fireball I'd done right before going outside were starting to hit with a vengeance. And I'm sure the two Long Island Iced Teas I'd consumed before that weren't helping either.

Sure, I was drunk off my ass, but even if I had been stone-cold sober, that kiss would have had me dropping trou and begging him to take me any way he wanted. I also had the feeling I should know this guy. Instead of making me wary of what was going on, it put me more at ease to think I knew the guy. It was dark outside, and I was otherwise occupied sucking his neck on the way inside and couldn't focus on anything other than getting myself and him naked.

The next thing I knew, we were in a room, and he was kicking the door shut as he fisted his hand in my hair and turned me so he could kiss me again. It wasn't a gentle kiss. In fact, it was almost brutal in its intensity. I reveled in it. My clit throbbed with each thrust of his tongue.

One of his hands slid under my shirt to cup my breast. He squeezed and kneaded the slight mound through my bra until I moaned into his mouth, surrendering myself to him completely.

Somehow, my shirt ended up on the floor along with his and his strong arms circled my body to hold me against his naked chest. My bra was the only thing preventing me from rubbing my nipples over his muscled chest. With a frustrated whimper, I tried to reach behind me to undo my bra, but his arm was over the clasp. He grunted and shoved the offending garment up over my tits with his other hand, never letting go of his hold around my body.

"Oh, God!"

When he dipped his head to latch onto one of my nipples, I came unglued. Arching into his touch wasn't enough. I needed to be naked so he could touch other parts of my body. And I desperately wanted to touch him.

He lifted me again, urging my legs around his hips. I could feel the ridge of his cock through my jeans and his and ground my cunt against it. Friction. I needed friction.

When I was on my back on the bed, he let me go long enough to whip my jeans off. He must have taken my panties and shoes with them because I found myself naked except for my socks and bra. Then his head was between my legs, and I forgot my own name. All I could do was scream.

The alcohol made me lightheaded, and that problem was compounded by pleasure like I'd never known existed. The room seemed to spin and spin until I was completely out of control. All I could do was hang on to his broad, muscled shoulders as he crawled up my body.

The tip of his cock entered my pussy in one hard shove, and we both cried out. There was an unexpected pain as he entered me, reminding me why I'd set out on this venture in the first Goddamned place. At nineteen, I was still a virgin. I'd hoped to give myself an early Christmas present by finding someone to fix that little problem. Looked like I'd managed. The problem was, it really hurt. I sucked in a breath, tensing up and gripping his hips with my thighs.

"What's wrong, sugar?" Were his words slurred? Between the haze of lust still enveloping me, the shock of the pain, and all the alcohol I'd consumed, I couldn't be sure. The point was he stopped moving.

"Just… just give me a minute," I gasped out.

"I hurt you?"

"No! I mean, yes, but it's easing."

"Too big for ya." I'd have thought those words

would have been said with a smugness that would have set my teeth on edge. Instead, he stroked my hair off my face and continued to kiss my jaw and chin until he found my mouth once again. Then he began those drugging kisses, building me back up to the point of madness once again.

He stayed perfectly still, though I could feel his heart throbbing through his chest as well as his dick. He tasted of whiskey and mint. Even if I'd been sober, the taste of him would have been just as intoxicating as any alcohol. Not because he'd been drinking. Because of the way he made me feel.

"Take a breath, sugar." His voice was smooth now, like he had more control than before. Which I wasn't sure I liked. I wanted him as out of control as I was. Though, I had to be grateful he'd paused the action. Past the pain of when he'd first entered me, the way he stretched my pussy burned, though the pain was replaced by a pleasurable ache. An ache that needed to be eased by the orgasm I knew was close by.

"Please," I begged in a whisper, "I need…"

"I know, sugar," he said near my ear. "Hold on to me. I'll make it good for you."

I did as he instructed, and he started to… *move*.

With wicked snaps of his hips, he pressed forward, sliding farther inside me until he was seated all the way. Then he slid out again. Then back in. The pain was gone and the burn fading. In their place was an unimaginable pleasure, one I had no hope of fighting.

"Oh, God… Oh, God!" I broke out in a sweat as the sensations built and built. There was a roaring in my ears that grew louder by the second. The man fucking me moved faster, but all I could focus on was the pleasure radiating from my clit and pussy as it spread through my thighs and belly.

Then it happened. With a scream, I came. It was like nothing I'd ever experienced before. No amount of masturbation had ever given me what I was experiencing now. My orgasm rushed through me with the force of a detonation. I thrashed under him, meeting each thrust of his hips with one of my own. My pussy clamped down on him, making the throbbing of his cock that much more intense inside me.

Somewhere in the haze of my surroundings, I heard this man bellow to the ceiling, his cock growing impossibly bigger only to pulse inside me over and over. He shuddered around me as his own body went slick with sweat. The last thing I remember before I passed out was his hoarse groan.

"Fuck... me..."

Chapter Two

Cyclone

Sweet baby Jesus in the manger, my head fucking hurt. And yeah, Jesus had very little to do with it. I'd debased myself all on my own. The hangover, I'd been expecting. What I wasn't expecting was the bare breast next to my mouth with the nipple just begging to be sucked. Without thinking, I snaked my tongue out and lapped at it.

Delicious.

The woman beneath me moaned, tunneling her fingers through my hair gently, almost tentatively. I took the nipple between my lips and sucked gently, loving the way it pebbled to my touch.

God, I wanted to fuck this woman again! I had vague memories of the pleasure I'd found with her the night before, but my head was having none of it. It felt like an ice pick stabbing into my temple.

With a groan, I moved to kiss between her delicate breasts before I looked up into her face... *and froze.*

She had a dreamy smile on her face, but her brows pinched together like she was in pain. Beautiful chestnut curls spread out like a halo over the pillow. Her eyes were closed, and she made a contented sound as she arched her back, offering her breast to me. She most definitely wasn't a club girl. In fact...

"Willa?"

She frowned.

I couldn't help but reach up to stroke the frown on her delicate lips. Then her cheek. "Hey, honey. Open your eyes for me."

Her lashes fluttered before she followed my instructions and opened her dark brown eyes to look straight into mine. Eyes filled with a mixture of pleasure and pain. Her lips parted on a gasp. Then she groaned, her hand going to her head.

"Oh, God…"

"Headache?" It was a stupid question to ask, but I really had nothing else at the moment. I was in shock because, really, this couldn't be happening.

"Yeah." She swallowed, then her eyes opened in alarm. "Sick…"

I rolled off her, pulling her up with me to sit up in the bed. She gave a weak whimper before scooting to the edge and running toward the bathroom. I knew how she felt. My stomach was rebelling too. I took several deep breaths, trying to calm my roiling stomach. This was a serious clusterfuck.

Willa. Trucker's daughter. Trucker, as in the road captain for Bones MC. Unless she'd somehow replaced the woman I'd been with all fucking night, I'd spent the entire night with the daughter of a truly massive man, fucking her senseless. Yeah. My life expectancy had just decreased dramatically. To make matters worse, I couldn't be sure I wouldn't seek her out in the future for more of what we'd done. Not only were the bits and pieces I remembered mind-blowing, I knew I wanted to experience this woman stone-cold sober, so I could enjoy every blistering second of fucking her sweet pussy.

My headache got worse.

The toilet flushed, and I hurried to sling on a pair of jeans as the woman in question stumbled out of the bathroom. She'd snagged one of my T-shirts from the bathroom to cover herself and kept her head down as she stood there. The only words I could use to describe the current situation was *fucking awkward*.

"You good?" It was a lame question.

"Yep." She didn't look at me, but crossed her arms over her chest and avoided my eyes. Her back was to the wall next to the bathroom, and she seemed to be trying to blend in with the flat surface. Which is when I noticed the condom wrappers.

There were at least six scattered over the floor. I guess that was something. Though I had no idea where I'd put what I'd used. Which was more than a little gross. But I was a guy and this was my space. The fact that it bothered me when it never would have before messed with my mind a little.

I looked back to Willa and had to shake my head. Which reminded me of the pounding headache I was trying to ignore. Never in my life had I seen a woman look so Goddamned sexy. She was small, with legs that seemed to go on for miles. All that curly hair fell in ringlets down her back nearly to her waist, surrounding her like a cape. Those dark brown eyes were large and round. Innocent. I had no doubt she'd never been in a situation like this in her life and probably never would be again.

She glanced up at me before lowering her gaze again. "What happens now?"

Yeah. That was the million-dollar question.

I took a deep breath before I replied. "Are you on any kind of birth control, Willa?" When she gasped and looked up at me with wide, shocked eyes I had my answer. I tried to keep my voice gentle when I felt anything but gentle. I wanted to kick my own ass. "We'll get something to keep you from getting pregnant in case I forgot protection."

"Seems like you used condoms." She indicated the opened packets on the floor. "I'm sure it'll be fine." Her naivety grated on my nerves. I had to remind myself none of this was her fault. I had no reason to be irritated with her. I was irritated because I was all kinds of stupid for letting this happen in the first Goddamned place and needed to lash out.

"Do you remember everything about last night, Willa? Because I sure the fuck don't. Only takes one time." I let my exasperation show despite knowing being harsh with her was a shit thing to do.

She flinched back, her face flushing. "No." Her voice was barely above a whisper. "I'm sorry. You're right. That was a stupid thing to say."

I sighed, feeling like a complete fucking asshole. I'd known Willa since she was a baby. I'd been a skinny teenager at the time, but I remembered Trucker carrying a very pregnant Helen from the back of that fucking eighties-model Winnebago with a knife sticking out of her belly. Mama had delivered Willa into the world and Helen had refused to name her until they'd caught the man who'd stabbed her. Not out of stubbornness, though. Out of fear.

That man's death was a legend in the club. They'd gotten the bastard so drunk the moonshine they fed him dribbled from his lips because he was unable to swallow. He'd probably have died on his own from alcohol poisoning if they'd let him be. But no one in Bones used hope as a tactic when it came to something like a man's death. Oh no.

It had been the coldest couple of weeks on record for the area when we'd struck. And by "we," I mean my dad, Cain, and the rest of the club. I was too young to participate. Me and my brother, Ice, had snooped in club business, watching and listening to everything we could. Looking back, I'm sure Data and Cain knew we were snooping. It wasn't long after that Dad had talked with us about being careful what we said in front of others and to never, under any circumstances, discuss anything associated with Bones with anyone outside of the club.

The guy had been blackout drunk. Unable to do anything but lie where they left him on the floor of the shack he'd been renting while looking for Helen. They'd left the doors and windows open, and the guy had frozen to death. Considering the fact he'd been trying to cut the baby from Helen's body to sell, I thought he'd gotten off too easy.

"You want me to take you to the pharmacy? I'll get you a morning after pill." I tried to soften my tone but wasn't certain I managed.

"No. I'm good. I can go myself."

I nodded my head only to wince as the pounding intensified. "Good. Just so you know, I'm clean. But if you still want to get tested, I'll pay for it." She nodded her head but didn't say anything. "You'll let me know if you, uh, you know, you need anything?" Could I be any more of a bastard?

"Yeah." She kept her arms crossed over her chest and all but bolted for the door, not bothering with her clothes. I'd have to get those back to her at some point. Preferably without Trucker knowing. Though my shirt swallowed her whole, I found myself tilting my head, staring at her retreating form, hoping to catch a glimpse of her ass as she fled.

That wasn't gonna work out well for me. Especially as I glanced at the sheets on my bed and saw a stain of blood. Yeah. I wasn't touching possibility because there was absolutely no way I'd taken Willa's virginity while so drunk I could barely remember anything. That was just too crass for words. If this situation didn't cost me my position as vice president of Bones for abusing my power over an innocent woman, it would certainly get me killed by

Trucker.

Well. If he decided to punish me, I'd take it like a man. Even if I had to stand there while the big bastard cut my Goddamned throat.

* * *

Willa

Oh, God. I was in so much trouble.

OK. So, this was salvageable. First thing I needed to do was go to the pharmacy. I could get Plan B over the counter easily enough. I believed Cyclone when he said he was clean. And he was right. I didn't remember enough about the previous night to be sure of anything. Well, other than the fact that we'd had sex.

Sweet God, we'd had sex!

I wished like anything I could remember it all. The flashes I had were surreal and unbelievable in how good the sex was. I could remember him working my body with a masterful touch, coaxing me into one orgasm after another until he'd simply demanded I come for him. And I had. Oh, how I had. For my first time, Cyclone had certainly made sure I'd had as much pleasure as humanly possible.

Had any other man besides Cyclone been cuddled on top of me when I woke, I'd probably have burst into a fit of giggles. Well. *After* I'd puked. Cyclone... terrified me. I had no idea why, but I'd seen the intense look he got sometimes. The way he focused on the enemy. Lord knew several of the old ladies had once had enemies. Cyclone had fought those enemies the same as every other member of Bones. The difference between him and everyone else was I got the feeling Cyclone enjoyed the violence.

Unfortunately, he was also the most beautiful man I'd ever seen. Sure, he was rugged and all that macho shit men seemed to embrace, but he was as handsome a man as ever I'd seen. Dark blond hair with a slightly darker beard framed his face. Intense hazel eyes seemed to see everything. Before he'd let his beard grow, when he'd kept stubble or shaved his face clean, he'd been obscenely good-looking. With the beard? Yeah. The man was devastating. And every single woman in the club had her eyes set on him. I was way too young to be able to hold my own with a man like him or to even keep his attention for longer than it took to take me to bed. Likely, he'd have forgotten about me by this time tomorrow.

I stumbled to my room. It was still early, and the clubhouse was quiet. Thank God. Doing the walk of shame in Cyclone's big T-shirt wasn't something I wanted anyone to witness. The club girls would be all over me and I wasn't ready for that.

As a rule, families of club members stayed away from the club girls. That prevented problems. While old ladies were generally easygoing and docile, when it came to protecting their claim on their men there wasn't one of them who couldn't be as vicious as those men. Even Suzie, Stunner's woman and Cain's daughter, and the sweetest person I'd ever met, had taken matters into her own hands when one of the newer club girls had made a play for Stunner after he'd been voted in as sergeant at arms for Bones. It hadn't been a beating per se, but that one swing of Suzie's bat had broken both bones in the woman's forearm. And Suzie had swung that bat with a smile.

So yeah. I wasn't ready for anyone to know what I'd been up to with Cyclone. Seemed like he wasn't too keen on anyone seeing me, either, and I didn't really blame him. I was at least fifteen years his junior, as well as the daughter of his road captain. I seriously doubted he wanted anyone finding out I'd spent the night with him.

I knew I needed to go to the pharmacy, but my head pounded, and my stomach was in knots. All I wanted to do was drink as much Gatorade as I could. Then find and take a bottle and a half of aspirin. Maybe then I'd feel human again.

Chapter Three

Cyclone
Six Weeks Later

"It's settled, then," Ice said with a grin. "Cheetah and Millie are both patched in." There were congratulations and applause. Both women had huge smiles on their faces. Millie looked up at Shadow, who dropped a kiss to her forehead. "Cheetah, unless you want to pass off the making of colors to someone else now, do your thing."

"I got this." Cheetah's smile was brilliant. The woman was in her mid-to-late-forties now, and very beautiful. As long as she'd been with the club, and as affectionate as she was with everyone -- she really was a hugger -- I'd never seen her with a man -- or woman for that matter -- in any kind of intimate fashion. Sure, Cheetah partied just as hard as everyone in the club, but sex didn't seem to factor into the equation. "And if Millie manages to talk Venus into patching over, I'll do her colors in hot pink." That got a laugh from everyone.

I glanced at my brother, and he gave me a nod and a grin. Yeah. We'd be approving any request from Venus if she decided to come be with her sister. I was glad to get this moving.

"Glad to see you men did this." Cain came forward to me and Ice. The rest of the club was giving Millie and Cheetah their congratulations, leaving me and Ice, along with a few of the other officers, to speak with Cain. He shook his head once. "Shoulda done it a long time ago. Guess I was too resistant to change."

"That why you resigned?" Ice had always been more sensitive to our dad's moods, while I was more in tune with our mother.

Cain shrugged. "Partly, maybe. I am getting too old to try to manage both Bones and ExFil. Since ExFil is what mostly funds everyone here, and most of Salvation's Bane depends on ExFil for work as well, I decided I could best serve everyone by keeping a hands-on approach to ExFil. Ain't sellin' the company, and you boys ain't quite ready to take that over."

I snorted. "Ain't speakin' for Ice, but I'm not sure I'd ever want to take over ExFil. I love workin' there, but the bureaucracy involved, especially when we get sent somewhere by the CIA, is more than I like to deal with."

"Well, that *and* you suck at bureaucracy." Ice grinned. "Last job you went on didn't go so well with the CIA officer in charge."

Cain actually chuckled. The man rarely showed any kind of affection or preference toward us when dealing with club business, and he'd gotten in my face over that incident. "I love you, son, but you will never be in charge of ExFil."

I barked out a laugh. "Well, thank God for that. After you pulled the stunt of putting me and Ice in charge of Bones, I was worried. I'd never willingly go against you, but I'd have fought you on that one."

Ice looked at me, his lips twitching as he fought a grin. "Ditto."

"Asshole."

"Need to talk to you, Cyclone." Cain jerked his head in the direction of the stairs. "My office." His mood was still somewhat light, but I could sense a shift. Whatever he needed to talk to me about was serious.

"You mean, *my* office." Ice smirked.

Cain scowled. "You're the president of Bones, you little shit. But the office is still mine."

Ice chuckled and raised his hands in surrender. "Must be why I'm still waiting to move all my shit in."

"Why don't you go see to your woman. Give me another grandbaby to spoil."

"Already on that one, Cain. I'll have her knocked up before you know it."

Cain gave a curt nod. "See that you do." He looked at me and his gaze hardened. "Come with me."

OK, this was different. I glanced at Ice and his expression was as puzzled as I felt. As I followed Cain down the hall, my gut tightened. Whatever this was about, it was fucking serious.

Once inside, Cain sat at his desk. "Close and lock the door, Cyclone." He never called us Cliff and Daniel now. Once we'd been given our road names, that's who we were to him. When I turned back, he nodded at the chair across from his desk. "Sit."

I did, crossing my ankle over the opposite knee. "What's going on?"

"You tell me." The order was barked like a drill sergeant. It was difficult not to flinch.

"Gonna have to give me a point of reference, Cain."

"Mama said there's something going on with Trucker's daughter, Willa. Said you'd know what and could fix it."

Several feelings shot through me. First and foremost was dread. But if I were honest, there was also an odd sense of anticipation that I had no business feeling.

"Mama said that." It wasn't a question. Cain didn't answer, just stared me down. Hard. I'd seen that look a few times in my life since coming to live at Bones. He didn't use it often but when he did, no one defied him. Not even me. "I'll take care of it."

"You'll tell me what the fuck went down so I can see if I can contain the damage."

I watched my father carefully, trying to gauge what I needed to do or say. "With all due respect, Cain, you made me vice president. This is something I need to fix on my own."

He slammed his hand down on the desk, standing to pace the length of the room. "If you've done something to Willa, Truck'll kill you and I won't be able to stop him. You know that, right?"

"Fully aware. I wouldn't lift a finger to defend myself, either. He has a right to defend his daughter as he sees fit."

"Then fuckin' tell me what the fuck happened!"

"That's between me and Willa, Cain." I had to stand my ground. Knowing Cain was trying to protect me, that he had my back as much as he could, was good to know, but I was the vice president of Bones. He needed to give me the respect of treating me as such. "I'll talk to her. See what the problem is."

Cain turned to face me then, his face thunderous. "The problem is, she's gone."

My gaze narrowed. Thinking back, I realized Trucker hadn't been at Church, which was unusual. Especially since everyone knew we were voting to not only patch in Millie and Cheetah, but to consider women to be patched in in the future.

"Gone?" I was hyper-focused on Cain now. That sense of anticipation turning to dread in a heartbeat.

"Yeah. Trucker said Helen had missed Willa day before yesterday. When she didn't call or text last night, Helen went looking for her. She wasn't in her room, and there was a note saying she was leaving for a while and would get in touch with them once she was settled."

"She's left Bones."

"Helen said she'd been acting odd for several days. She was worried about Willa. So was Trucker."

"They talk to Mama?"

Cain leveled me a hard look. "If they had, trust me when I say you'd most definitely know it."

"I'll get Data to track her cell. I'll find her."

"You better." Cain pointed an accusing finger at me. "When you do, you better fucking make whatever happened between the two of you right. You don't, vice president of Bones or not, grown-ass man or not, you'll fuckin' answer to me. Worse, you'll answer to Trucker."

"I hear you."

"Yeah? Because after you answer to both of us you'll have to answer to Angel. If she cries, Daniel, if you make your mother cry…" The threat was implied but could not be overstated.

"Understood, sir." It was the only way to answer my father with something this serious.

* * *

Willa

"License and registration, please."

I was in a world of trouble. I'd been so preoccupied trying to ignore my personal problems I hadn't been paying attention to anything but the traffic around me. Yeah, I'd passed a few vehicles, but there were also cars that had passed me.

The North Carolina state trooper stood next to my car at the driver's side looking appropriately menacing. He frowned as I retrieved the requested documents, my license from my wallet and the car registration from the glove compartment.

He took both items and stalked back to his car. It

had been six weeks since my encounter with Cyclone and no matter what I did, I couldn't move past it. Probably because he'd been my first. He'd been the man to take my virginity and it had been glorious. Well, what I could remember of it anyway. Bits and pieces of the night came back to me in the ensuing days, and I'd come to four conclusions.

First, I was certain it had been the best night of my life thus far. Second, I wanted a repeat. Third, there was no way I was getting a repeat. Fourth, there was no way I could see Cyclone with one of the other women in the club. Or anyone else for that matter. Which all added up to me needing a break from Somerset.

"Do you know what the speed limit in this area is, ma'am?"

My attention snapped back to the problem at hand. Which was that North Carolina officer. "I…" I glanced at my GPS which indicated the speed limit on the interstate where we were. "Sixty?"

He scowled at me. "Please step out of the car."

"What's going on?"

"Please step out of the car," he repeated, none too gently.

I swallowed hard and did as he ordered.

Once I was out, he shut my car door. "Turn around and face the vehicle. Put your hands on the hood."

"I don't understand what's happening. Are you *arresting* me?" My heart pounded and I broke out in a sweat. Tears threatened and I wished like hell I'd called my mother while I'd waited on the officer to come back to the car. At least they'd know something was wrong.

"Ma'am, I clocked you doing ninety-eight miles

an hour. My radar gun's been calibrated recently, but even I found that hard to believe, so I paced you for over a mile to verify what I was seeing before I hit my lights."

"I… *ninety-eight*?" My voice squeaked. Dear God. I was in so much trouble…

"That's correct. Were you even paying attention to anything? I was right behind you, and you never let off the gas."

When I just stared at him, he took my shoulder and spun me around before patting me down. Once done, he took my upper arm, urged me in the direction of his car, put me in the back seat, then started reading me my rights.

After that, things were kind of a blur. I have no idea if he shut my car off or got my purse and wallet or my phone. I wanted to cry, but I was too scared to do anything other than sit there in shock.

He got in the car and turned to face me. "If you're running from something, you need to tell me now, ma'am. I'm not about punishing someone who's trying to get away from a bad situation, but the speed you were driving isn't safe for you or other drivers around you."

"No," I said quietly. "I didn't realize I was going so fast."

"You were nearly *forty* miles over the speed limit." He looked as stern and cross as any cop would in his position. "I'm charging you with reckless driving. I'll have your car towed. Once we get to the station, you can call someone to come get you and get the car out of impound."

"I'm not from here, sir. I don't have anyone to call."

"Do you have family?"

"I do, but they're all in Kentucky. I was, uh, on a trip."

"Then you can call Kentucky once we get to the police station."

"My phone is in my car with my wallet."

"I'll get your phone and your wallet. They'll be checked at the station, but they'll let you make a call."

"How long will I have to stay there?"

"Until someone comes to pick you up. I'm sorry, ma'am, but I'm doing this for your own good. At seventy, I'd have given you a citation and let you go -- but ninety-eight? You're going to get yourself killed. Or, worse, kill someone else. Do you understand?"

I blinked several times, trying not to cry. "Yes, sir."

"Good. I'll be right back."

He went to my car, turned it off and put a tag on the driver's door before he returned with my wallet, phone, and keys. After doing a quick inventory, he sealed it in a bag with my phone and my keys.

"I locked your car. I'm putting an immediate suspension on your license in the state of North Carolina pending a hearing."

"I'm so sorry, officer. I'm sorry."

"I understand. I hope you understand my job is to keep everyone driving this road as safe as I can. That includes you."

"Yes, sir."

Chapter Four

Cyclone

"What the fuck is she doing in North Carolina?" I realized the situation I'd gotten me and Willa into wasn't ideal, but her discomfort was no reason to take off and worry her parents. She wasn't in an unsafe situation. There was no way I'd ever hurt Willa -- or any woman for that matter -- simply because we'd both been drunk and not considering it wasn't a good idea for us to be behaving like we did. At worst, seeing each other would be a bit awkward for a while, but it was just sex. Most adults had sex at some point in their life. Besides, even if she felt unsafe or thought I'd use my position to harm her in any way, all she had to do was go to her daddy and Trucker'd take care of me. And I'd be dead.

"Not sure." Data was moving his mouse from one screen to another, alternately typing and clicking until he got the information he wanted. "Her phone's at the Haywood County Jail. Looks like her car's been impounded."

"Fuck!" I scrubbed a hand over my face. "What do they have her on?"

Data's face was hard, his brows knit together. "Speeding and reckless driving. She was arrested a couple hours ago. They're still processing her. Looks like she was doing ninety-eight in a sixty."

"And they arrested her for that? I realize North Carolina is real hard-ass with shit like that, but actually *arresting* her seems a bit of an overkill."

Data shook his head. "Not sure, brother. Like I said, she's still in processing."

"Reach out to them. Make her bail so she can come home."

"I can make her bail, but she's gonna need someone to go get her. They've suspended her license pending her trial date."

I took a deep breath, then let it out slowly. Calm. I needed calm. "Just pay her bail. Get her a taxi to a hotel and send the info to my phone. And send me a virtual key so I can get in when I get there."

"Maybe you should send Trucker after her. Or ask Ice and Dawn. Cain and Angel would go, too. You don't seem to be in the best frame of mind for the job."

"You're about three seconds away from pissing me the fuck off, Data. I realize I'm a couple decades younger than you, but I'm capable of rounding up one small woman on my own."

"Hey. Ain't sayin' you aren't capable. Just sayin' you don't want to scare the girl to death or Trucker'll have your hide."

"If one more person reminds me how Willa is Trucker's little darlin'. I think I'll puke." I muttered the complaint under my breath, but it was really becoming a problem. Yes, I'd fucked up. I got it. The reminder that my neck was on the line was not needed. Besides that, I already felt bad about the whole thing. Well, not the *whole* thing. That night I'd spent with Willa would haunt me for the rest of my life. The woman was all kinds of special. So sweet and innocent, with a willingness to let me corrupt her and never question anything I did. She'd followed where I led and hadn't looked back.

"What happened between you and Willa, Cyclone?" Data's wife, Zora, narrowed her eyes at me.

I mimicked her expression just to piss her off. "What makes you think anything happened between me and Willa?"

Zora rolled her eyes. "Well, she didn't leave the

club to go *find* herself or whatever excuse she gave Trucker and Helen. The rumor is she was seen leaving your room in the wee hours of the morning a few weeks ago wearing nothing but a very oversized T-shirt."

"That's the rumor, huh?"

She shrugged. "Well, that, *and* I did some digging. Security cameras are a bitch when you're trying to hide an illicit affair."

"Zora…" Data glanced at his wife.

She just lifted her chin stubbornly. "It's true. You saw it same as me. Though, I have no idea why he took Willa to *his* room instead of hers or someplace neutral if he didn't intend to make her his."

Data scrubbed a hand over his beard. "Honey, we talked about this. Pretty sure both of them were more than a little drunk."

"So? Is that any excuse for him to avoid her for weeks afterward? How would you feel if he'd done it to Eleanor or Alice?"

"No, baby." Data reached over to squeeze Zora's knee. "It's not an excuse. And you know I'd kill him if it had been one of the girls." Data didn't look at me and I knew that was on purpose. He was trying to diffuse the situation with me and Zora, but yeah. I was very much in the wrong.

Zora looked me in the eyes, obviously wanting to drive her point home. "She's a good girl, Cyclone. If you don't want her, that's fine, but don't ignore her like she's nothing. I get that you don't love her or feel anything other than friendship for her. You watched her grow up so I'm sure the situation isn't comfortable, but she deserves for you to acknowledge whatever happened between you." She stabbed me in the chest hard with her finger. "You make it right."

"I will. Which is why I'm going to get her."

Before Zora could continue to chastise me, my phone buzzed in my back pocket. Being tied to a fucking phone was one thing about being vice president I fucking hated. With an annoyed huff, I pulled the thing out and checked the screen... and frowned.

"Data?" I turned the screen so he could see the number calling me. "That Willa's number?"

His eyes widened but it was Zora who answered me. "Yes, that's her. Answer it, Cyclone." It was a command, pure and simple.

I gave her a look but answered the call. "Willa?"

There was a silence before she spoke. "Uh, Bohannon?"

"No, honey. It's Cyclone."

"Daniel? Why are you answering Bohannon's phone?" I remember chastising the club girl for using my given name the night of the party. It never occurred to me to even correct Willa.

"It's the club phone, honey. I got it when I was elected vice president. You good?" It was a testament to how off-balance she was that she called me Daniel instead of Cyclone. She definitely wasn't expecting me to answer.

"*Déjà vu*," she muttered before replying in a stronger voice. "Yes. I'm good. I, uh, need someone to, uh," she cleared her throat, "come to North Carolina and pick me up."

"Yeah. I know. Your mom got worried when she found you were gone, so Data tracked your phone. What the hell were you thinking, going that fast? And in North Carolina?"

"I'm sorry, OK?" She raised her voice, but I could hear the slight wobble. "I didn't mean to. I had a lot on my mind and was just… *driving*."

"Cyclone…" Data stood and gripped my shoulder. "Rein it in or give me the fuckin' phone."

He looked as furious as I felt. Both of us were angry at me. I took a deep breath. "Sorry, Willa."

"Can you just tell Calliope or Cotton I need their help, please? I tried to call both of them, but it went straight to voicemail."

"Yeah, they've gone to Evansville to be with Blossom after she has that surgery on her foot."

"Shit. I forgot." She sighed heavily before continuing. "Would you mind maybe telling my dad? I didn't want to call him and Mom, but I'm not sure they'll let me call someone else since I actually talked to someone this time."

"I'm leaving in fifteen minutes to come after you, honey. Data's gonna work on getting you out and to a hotel. You can rest and get something to eat while I get there. Then I'll bring you home."

There was a pause. "I don't want you coming for me, Cyclone." There was a slight wobble to her voice, but she sounded almost angry as she made her wishes known. "Please send someone else."

"Sorry, honey. It's me you're gettin'. Just sit tight. I'll get you home. And we've got a lot to talk about."

I caught a muttered, "Stubborn bastard," before I ended the call. I shot off a text to Ice. He needed to know where I was going. Then I turned my attention back to Data. "Once you have arrangements made, send it to my phone. I'll also need an address to put in my maps."

"All over it."

"Cyclone." Zora wasn't letting me ignore her no matter how badly I wanted to. "You hurt her again, I won't go to Ice or even Trucker. I'll go straight to

Helen. After everything she'd had to go through to get Willa into this world..." Zora closed her eyes and inhaled for patience. Even I could see how she was trying to hold on to her temper. "Then to have the threat of her own personal monster coming back for her and the baby? Helen was so traumatized she wouldn't even name the child for fear of the bad luck it might bring them both. Well, if you think you're gonna be in trouble with Trucker, just wait until Helen gets ahold of you."

"Yeah. Copy that." I tried to keep the bite out of my voice. I figured I'd already pushed it far enough with the woman. Data would only let me get by with so much. I shook my head. "Sorry, Zora. I'm only irritated at you because you're a hundred percent right."

She raised an eyebrow. "Oh, I know. At least you better know. I'm not saying you have to make Willa your old lady or anything. But you need to respect her. No matter how uncomfortable you are with what happened. Have you even checked on her since then?"

I winced. "No. Tried to keep my distance."

"I see. I suppose you did it because you believe you're so irresistible to women she'll cling or something. Got news for you, big guy. You're not nearly as magnetic as you want to think. Most of the women here want you because of the power you represent, but I think you know that."

"I don't need a lecture from you, Zora. I'm aware the club girls see a single vice president as their ticket to ruling the roost around here. And, no, I don't want a woman of my own. Not yet anyway. I've got to establish myself as an authority figure in Bones, as well as learn a whole helluva lot before I even think about bringing a woman into my life permanently."

"Did she indicate she expected more from you than one night?" Zora wasn't letting this go. She intended to drive her point home and I honestly couldn't blame her.

"No. She didn't. And you're right. I should have checked on her. I offered help if she needed it, but I should have followed up and made sure she was all right."

"You absolutely should have." She leaned back in her chair, never taking her eyes off me. "I trust that's a mistake you won't make again."

"No, Zora." I didn't even try to keep the exasperation from my voice. "I'm not a complete dumbass. Now, while I realize you're looking out for Willa, you've pushed me as far as I'm going to let you. I fucked up. I freely admit that. And I'm going to fix my fuckup. But I'm still the vice president of this club and you're an old lady. That gives you liberties, but enough is enough."

She stood so suddenly her chair rolled back several inches. Then Data's tiny wife marched up to me and poked a finger into my chest hard enough to make me pay attention. "*Wrong*. It's not nearly enough, Cyclone. Not *nearly* enough."

Chapter Five
Willa

I couldn't sit still. They'd put me in a holding cell with a couple other women, but I was the only one who seemed on edge. The other two were watching me with smirks on their faces.

"I take it you've never been arrested before?" one of them asked as she popped her gum.

I shook my head without looking at her. "No. But that's not the problem," I muttered. While it wasn't exactly what I'd call comfortable sitting in a county jail, I'd rather stay here for days -- weeks even -- than face Cyclone. The good news was if he was coming to get me himself, it would be several hours at minimum before he got here. I just wanted out of here so I could wrap up in a big fuzzy blanket and contemplate my life choices.

"You afraid your daddy'll whup your ass?" The other one grinned like it was all some kind of big joke.

I snorted. "If only." They looked at each other. One of them rolled her eyes, but I tried not to look at either of them. "My dad's the least of my problems."

"Willa Norvac?" A woman in a light brown uniform approached the cell.

"Yes, ma'am." I stopped my pacing and turned to face her. There was no way Cyclone could have gotten here this fast.

"Your bail's been posted, honey. Come with me."

"I... but I can't drive. The state trooper who brought me in said my license was suspended immediately until I had my court date."

"That's correct. The person who paid your bail also paid for a cab to a hotel until someone comes to pick you up. You can check with the hotel when you get there, but I'm pretty sure your room's taken care of, too."

I nodded. Maybe Cyclone had sent my dad after all. One could hope. "Thank you."

She opened the cell door and I stepped out. Once the door slid shut, I followed the woman to the processing area once more. She handed me the bag with my things and instructed me to do an inventory. When I'd finished, I signed a form to take possession of it all and she escorted me outside. The taxi was waiting.

"Have a better night, honey," she said with a gentle smile. "Just make sure to slow down and pay attention from now on."

"Yes, ma'am." I didn't point out that I wouldn't be driving for the foreseeable future. "Thank you."

Once I was inside the taxi, we sped off. The guy tried to make small talk, but I was doing my best to stave off a panic attack. If I could hold it together for a little while longer, I could fall apart in private.

"Seems like you had an eventful evening." The guy grinned. He glanced at me every now and then through the rearview mirror. I didn't respond. *Couldn't* respond, not and keep my composure. I was trembling where I sat thinking about the coming confrontation. How was I going to get through this? I was sure I was making it out to be worse than it really was, but honestly, my emotions were off-the-charts chaotic.

The driver pulled up under an awning for a chain hotel. Nothing fancy, but reputable and nice. "Here we are."

The guy had continued to chat the whole trip. Even though I hadn't said much, he hadn't seemed to mind. Thank God it was only a fifteen-minute ride. By the time I stepped out of the cab, I was so wound up I felt like my hair was standing on end.

Sure enough, I had a room reserved and a payment method on file. Someone -- presumably at Bones -- had reserved a suite. Two rooms with one king-size bed and a sleeper sofa. Which meant Cyclone -- or whomever was on the way -- was planning on staying in the same room with me until they'd rested and were ready to head back. I was still holding out hope he'd give in and send someone else. The reminder I'd have to face someone soon didn't ease my anxiety.

I'd packed some clothing, but everything was in a suitcase -- in the trunk of my car. Even though I couldn't change clothes, I still wanted a shower. I felt grimy and dirty.

The bathroom was spacious and had both a shower and a deep, jetted tub. For the first time since I'd been stopped by that police officer, I started to calm down slightly. The simple prospect of a warm bath in a jacuzzi where the jets could pound my aching muscles for a while was welcome.

Being careful not to get the water too hot, even though I really wanted the temperature as hot as I could stand it, I ran the bath and stripped while the tub was filling. I'd just turned off the water when my phone trilled from the bathroom vanity.

I ignored the call, letting it go to voicemail. Whoever it was would leave a message if it was important. But the phone rang again. And a third time. Which was when I realized I was going to have to answer it because the caller wasn't going away.

I cringed when I saw Bohannon's name on the screen. I hadn't had a chance to change the contact name from Bohannon to Cyclone yet. He was the very last person I wanted to talk to right now. I thought about turning my phone off but knew doing so would only get me in more trouble than I was already in. God knew I didn't need more trouble. I was in over my head as it was. With a sigh of resignation, I picked up the phone -- which was now starting on the fifth call -- and answered it.

"Hello?"

"Why didn't you answer the phone?" His clipped demand made me cringe. I'd lived my whole life in the club and could hold my own against anyone there. Normally I wasn't the shrinking violet type. I had fire when I needed to, but these last few weeks had thrown me. I was dejected, uncertain, off-balance, and more than a little scared.

"I-I just got to the hotel. I left my phone in the bathroom." Not a lie.

There was a beat of silence before he continued. "Sorry I snapped. I was, uh, concerned when you didn't answer. You good?"

"Yep." Thankfully, he couldn't see me cringe, because I most definitely was not good. Physically, I was OK. Mentally? Not so much.

"Seems we've had that exchange before, huh?" When I didn't say anything, he continued. "I'm about three hours out, honey. Data gave me the hotel information and I've got a digital key, so don't be alarmed when I let myself in."

"Please don't call me honey." I couldn't make myself put any force behind my words. Mainly because, even though he was still several hours away and not right in front of me, he still intimidated me. Those feelings were more a state of mind for me because, until that night six weeks ago, I had rarely interacted with Cyclone. He was there, but off-limits. Same as I was off-limits to him, unspoken though it was. He had been a prospect, then a patched member of Bones. I was the daughter of an officer in Bones, not a club girl. Even though he was also family of an officer, he was so much older than me we'd never had a reason to interact.

"Yeah." He sounded tired. Or maybe resigned? "Sorry. I'm trying to be gentle and not too overbearing. Data and Zora thought I might frighten you if I didn't tone down my personality a bit."

When he didn't say anything more, I plucked up my courage and pushed him a little. "I'd like to take a bath and I need to see if I can get some stuff delivered. I don't have any clean clothes."

"Why not?" That bossy, demanding tone was back. This was definitely the vice president of a powerful MC I was talking to now. Not the man who was trying not to frighten me.

"My suitcase is in the trunk of my car and the car is impounded."

He grunted. "Get in touch with Zora. She'll take care of it."

"OK." I wouldn't be getting anyone else to do that stuff for me, but it wouldn't do any good telling him that. The path of least resistance was to tell him I'd be a good little girl and do what he said, then do whatever the fuck I wanted.

Again, there was a silence. I could all but see him narrowing his eyes at me. "I'll tell Zora to call you. She'll probably be able to anticipate what you need, but I don't want her to miss anything. We won't be heading back tonight, obviously. So I want you to have everything you'll need." Yeah. He knew what I was about.

"I can take care of it. You're driving. If you don't concentrate, you'll end up in the same position I'm in."

That came out more annoyed than I thought I was capable of with Cyclone. The man was seriously pushing all my buttons and I hated he could get to me this easily. "I know you think I'm not capable of taking care of myself but I am. I don't need Zora to buy things for me with club money. I have a job and money of my own."

"Huh. You can push back. Who knew?" Did he sound... amused? Was he trying to push me over the edge?

"Am I some kind of entertainment for you? Is this all a big-ass joke?" Now my temper was spiking.

"Not at all, Willa. Like I told you before. You and I have things to discuss, and we need to be equals to do it. For whatever reason, you don't see yourself as my equal right now. It's my job to get you there."

Yeah, my temper was redlining. "Bastard," I muttered.

"Unquestionably. So hold on to all the emotions you've got running around inside you until I get there. Then we'll have it out. *As equals.*"

"I'm taking a bath, then I'm going to lie down. As I'm sure you realize, I've not had the best of days."

"Good. I'll text you when I get there so you're not startled when I walk in on you."

I ended the call without saying goodbye because I simply couldn't say another word to the asshole without completely losing my shit. If I lost my shit, I knew I'd cry, and I wasn't going to do that. Not in front of him. As close to tears as I'd been before his call, now I was good and pissed. Why? Beat the fuck outta me. He hadn't said anything overt, but his attitude was so fucking smug! He was manipulating me into getting what he wanted. In this case, he wanted a certain emotional response. Anger over intimidation. What pissed me off was, it had worked. Even worse? He was right. In order to deal with him and this whole fucked-up situation, I needed to see us as equals. And I didn't.

"Ugh!" I yelled, not caring if anyone heard me. Surely to God the walls in a two-room suite would be thick enough to muffle the sound. I picked up the tiny complimentary bar of soap and threw it against the door. It wasn't much, but the emotional explosion helped me center myself and gain back a bit more of my backbone. After several weeks of self-pity and generally being down in the dumps, it kind of felt good. Just add it to the list of things that aggravated me about Cyclone.

While I was in the bath, I pulled up an app on my phone for a local store that delivered and started shopping for basic essentials. A change of clothes from top to bottom, toiletries, and some snacks. OK, *lots* of snacks. I had a four-pound tub of peanut butter and a forty-eight-ounce jar of grape jelly in the cart and my mouth was simply to God *watering*. And a half a gallon of milk. And a case of Coke Zero. And a big-ass barrel of fucking cheese balls.

Fuck.

I was about to place my order when my mom's name popped up on my phone screen to FaceTime. No way I was touching that. So I declined, then shot off a text.

Me: *In the bathtub. What's up?*

Mom: *Zora said you needed some clothes and stuff for an overnight stay. She said to put them in your cart and she'd take it from there.*

Mom: *Everything OK?*

How to answer that?

Me: *I know she told you what happened.*

Mom: *Yes. But I know there's something else going on. Tell me?*

Me: *I don't want to talk about it right now. I'm fine.*

I knew that wouldn't deter my mother, but I hoped she'd back off for a while. She'd get it out of me eventually -- it wasn't like I could keep my secret forever -- but I needed some more time. Plus, I had the "conversation" coming up with Cyclone. Talking about this with my mother wasn't high on my list of things I was just itching to do.

Mom: *Baby, if it's something I can help with, you know I will. Is it Cyclone? I know something happened between you two.*

How the fuck did she know that? I'd been very careful sneaking back to my room without anyone seeing me. Unless…

Me: *Who ratted me out?*

My temper was starting to redline again. Even if someone saw me, it wasn't their Goddamned business! If it was a club girl, I'd go medieval on her skank ass.

Mom: *Zora told me and made me promise not to tell your father. That's between you, him, and Cyclone. I don't care about any of that. I only care about you.*

That was my mother. She was always so gentle with everyone. She didn't like confrontation, and was always the one trying to smooth things over.

Me: *I'm fine, Mom. I just need some space and time to think. Besides, you know I like road trips.*

Mom: *I'm here if you need me, sweetie. My first loyalty is to my kids before anyone else. I will always take your side on anything. Your father will too. I hope you know that.*

Me: *I do. Thanks, Mom. But I promise I'm fine.*

Mom: *Good. Put the things in your cart and text Zora which app you're using. She'll take it from there.*

Me: *I can buy my own things.*

Mom: *I know. Since you won't let me help with anything else, I'm asking you to let me help with this.*

That was my mother. I knew from experience she meant every word. I also knew she'd get the whole story out of me sooner than I wanted. Because she was my mom.

An hour later, two of everything I'd ordered arrived. Along with two boxes of the Christmas cakes I loved so much. The regular-size ones. Not the jumbo ones. Because the jumbo ones didn't taste the same. So, yeah. I knew I was busted all the way around. There was no way Zora hadn't figured out my secret. Not with the additions to my order.

I groaned, falling to my back on the bed. Though I had at least a day before I had to face my mom and dad, I only had a couple hours to figure out what I was going to say to Cyclone. And I had to say something because by the time we got home, everyone in the stupid club would know what was going on because this shit never stayed quiet. Shit just got real.

Chapter Six

Cyclone

It took me close to four hours to reach the hotel and Willa. Longer than it should have because I took my time. I needed to figure out how I was going to handle this situation without hurting Willa or pissing her off too badly. Her getting angry was fine. It let me know she wasn't afraid to express herself and that she wasn't frightened of me. Pissing her off too much would only push her away, and she needed to come home.

If she refused to leave with me, I'd have to get Trucker to come get her, and he'd likely give me my beating here rather than in our home compound. Because, yeah. No matter what happened in the next couple of days, I'd resigned myself to a beating. Which meant my position in the club was going to be called into question because I absolutely would not defend myself, and this club needed strong leaders. Not pussies who wouldn't fight.

Pulling into the parking lot, I exhaled a long breath. Normally, driving a cage, I'd want to get there and back as quickly as possible. Though I didn't mind a chilly ride on my bike, I was sure Willa wouldn't appreciate having to ride behind me. I'd taken an F-150 so she'd be comfortable. I had the feeling there was more to this whole situation than Willa being upset, because I hadn't sought her out after that one explosive night.

Fuck. Just thinking about the night we'd spent together got me hard as fucking steel. True, there were parts that were hazy and try as I might I didn't have real clarity, but I'd literally fucked her all night long. The only thing that was completely clear was that it had been fucking blissful.

I sat in the truck for a good fifteen minutes before finally manning up and sending Willa the text I'd promised. The last thing I wanted to do was scare her any worse than she probably already was. What I had to figure out was what had spooked her. Obviously, staying away from her had been a mistake, but how did I get her to tell me why she'd run? More importantly, how did I fix it?

One thing at a time. First, I'd go to her room and check on her. Make sure she was OK. Then I'd get her something to eat if she was hungry. After that, I'd shower and get some rest. Tomorrow, we'd talk. I'd get her to tell me what was going on, then I'd help her fix it. Once she felt better about her situation, we'd head home.

Simple.

The suite Zora had secured for Willa was on the top floor. Though I'd texted Willa, I still knocked on the door before using my phone to unlock the door and step inside.

"Willa?" She didn't answer, but her small form moved from the bedroom to the doorway of the living area. She'd piled a metric crap-ton of junk food on the counter by the tiny refrigerator. And I mean she was fucking *serious* about the junk food.

She was dressed in an oversized sleep shirt and black leggings. Thick fuzzy socks were on her feet. She leaned against the door, looking anywhere but at me, standing on one foot while the other one rubbed at the back of the opposite ankle.

"Hey." I set my bag on the floor before turning my full attention to her.

"Hey." Her voice was small, and she wrapped her arms around herself.

For long moments we stood there. I had no idea what to say, and she looked like she didn't want me anywhere near her.

The bathroom was in the bedroom part of the suite, which meant I'd have to invade her territory. I took a deep breath and pointed through the open doorway to the bathroom. "Do you mind if I clean up?"

Without a word, she turned and crossed to a chair on the other side of the room, putting the bed between us. Well. Rome wasn't built in a day.

I snagged a change of clothes from my bag before heading to the bathroom. I took my time in the shower, enjoying the heat on my muscles after the ride in that fucking cage. Maybe I'd have been just as sore and stiff if I'd ridden my bike, but I didn't think so. I was used to long rides. Enjoyed them. As I dried and dressed, I scowled. I'd come four hours to get Willa and she hadn't said a fucking word to me when I'd gotten here. My ire built further when I opened the door to find her nowhere in sight.

"Willa?" I called out to her, but she didn't answer. If she'd left the suite, I was going to spank her ass no matter how much trouble it got me in when we got back to Kentucky. "Willa!"

I stormed into the next room and came up short. She sat in a chair with her knees to her chest looking out the window. She didn't turn her head or acknowledge me in any way. There was no way she hadn't heard me, so this was deliberate. I ground my teeth in frustration.

"Willa, I can't help you if you won't talk to me."

When she spoke, her voice was soft. Small. Lost. *Fuck*. "What do you plan on doing with your life, Cyclone?"

OK, that came out of nowhere. I took a careful step toward her, even though she was facing away from me. I didn't want to startle her, though she could probably see my reflection in the glass. "I'll continue to work at ExFil and help Cain all I can while helping my brother lead Bones. It worked for Cain. It will work for me and Ice too."

"What about besides that? What about a family?"

I shrugged, not sure where she was going with this. "Hadn't really planned on having a family other than Bones. I mean, I have my parents and brothers and sisters, but I hadn't really thought about anything else.

She turned to look at me then, her wide, brown eyes glistening with unshed tears, but her face was an expressionless mask. "I'm pregnant, Cyclone."

The silence stretched on while I processed what she was saying. Pregnant. Willa. I shook my head once, not truly understanding her words. "OK." The statement didn't compute, like, at all. "You're pregnant. I'm sure Trucker and Helen will be overjoyed. I mean, unless you were going someplace to have an abortion?" Everything inside me rebelled at... something. The idea that she was pregnant? The fact she had a choice to terminate the pregnancy? I was a believer that a woman needed to be able to make her own choices, but I didn't want Willa to get an abortion. And I couldn't figure out why.

Her expression hardened. "No, dumbass," she snapped. "I'm not going someplace to have a fucking abortion. How can you be so obtuse?" Instead of the scared waif who'd run from my bedroom six weeks before or the emotionless, resigned woman I'd first seen when I got inside the hotel room, this Willa was full of fire. A strong protector for the child she carried.

The transition made me sit up and take notice. Did the same for my cock, too.

"I wasn't trying to be insensitive, Willa. What the fuck is going on? This is about more than you being pregnant. Having a baby isn't the end of the world and if you really don't want the child you can get rid of it."

She closed her eyes and took a deep breath. If I had to read her expression, I'd say she was inhaling for patience. When she opened her eyes again, they were filled with unadulterated *fury*. "You're the father, Cyclone. You. Doesn't take a genius to figure that out and you're not completely stupid." She held my gaze with her force of will alone. "I'm pregnant with your child, Cyclone." If the tone of her voice and the angry fire she was spitting at me were accurate, she wasn't happy about the situation. And not because she was pregnant. She didn't want me as the father. Which suited me just fine. It did! Really!

I shook my head. "You got the morning after pill. Right?"

She rolled her eyes, clearly exasperated. Like she wanted to go, *Duh, dumbass*! "I did. But I was hungover the morning I snuck out of your room back to my own. So I didn't go to the pharmacy until the next day. Apparently, the longer you wait, the less likely the pill is to work, and it already started at only sixty-five percent efficacy. I had little better than a fifty-fifty chance it would work, and I lost."

Scrubbing a hand over my mouth, I sat on the couch next to Willa's chair, never taking my eyes off her. "Pregnant."

She stuck her chin up and her frown deepened. "Yep. Pregnant. You know. Knocked up. Bun in the oven. Preggers. Prego."

When she would have continued, I shot her a

look. "I know what it means, Willa."

I waited for the panic I knew would follow to set in like a clue-by-four between my eyes. And waited. I stared hard at Willa, knowing she was right but not being able to process the whole situation. Her little pixie face reminded me of an angry Tinkerbell. I could all but see her arms at her sides, hands balled into fists as she stomped a tiny foot on the ground while fairy dust scattered around her.

A grin split my face. Holy shit. "Pregnant."

"It's not funny, you bastard!" She shot to her feet and kicked my shin. "Fucker!" Then she winced, not putting her foot back down. Obviously it had hurt her toes.

"I wasn't laughing at you, honey. Honest." My grin grew wider. "Come here." I held out a hand to her.

"You're delusional if you think I'm touching you right now. Not unless it's to stab your eyes out with a spork!"

I stood and reached for her, not missing the fact that she didn't pull back. Once she was in my arms, I rested my chin on the top of her head with my arms tightly around her. "I'm not making fun of you, Willa." I tried to rein it in, as Data had told me to do. Tried to sound gentle and compassionate and understanding. "Not at all. I'm laughing at myself."

"Why would you do that?" It was more of a demand than a question. She didn't pull away or even look up and her words were muffled against my shirt.

"Because the thought of you pregnant with my baby didn't send me running in a screaming frenzy to the fuckin' hills? Because your daddy's gonna kill my fuckin' ass, then resurrect me so he can do it again? Several times. He'll probably make an Olympic sport out of finding ways to make my death as miserable as possible. And you know what?" I waited until she looked up at me with angry, glistening eyes before speaking again. "It's worth it."

She frowned. "Why would you say that, Cyclone? You don't want a woman. Everyone says so. Why would me having your baby make you smile?" The longer she talked, the more thunderous her expression became. "Is this some kind of power trip for you? 'Cause your little guys can fucking swim?" She shoved out of my arms and stalked away, back toward the bedroom. "What a fucking asshole," she muttered as she disappeared through the open door.

"This isn't a power trip, Willa." I tried to smother my grin. "I'll be honest with you. I'm not sure why it makes me smile, you being pregnant with my baby, but it does."

"Well, it doesn't make me smile!" She whirled around where she stood next to the bed, pointing a finger at me. "You didn't want anything to do with me! Now you're happy about this? Ugh! You're such a bastard!"

I blinked several times while I tried to get a grip on reality here. There was no way in hell I should be happy about this. None whatsoever. Not only was she right that I didn't want a woman, but a baby would tie us together forever…

And there went my cock. Fucking bastard sprang hard almost instantly at the thought of her being in my life permanently. Not as my woman or anything, but I liked knowing she'd always be there. Which only led to more questions. Fuck.

No! I needed to focus on all the reasons this was a bad idea. I didn't want a kid. Not yet anyway.

"You're right. Look, honey. I get it. I'm sorry."

I reached out and tried to take her hand, but she shook it away.

"No." She stepped away, her voice quaking with emotion. "You don't get to touch me anymore."

I felt a pang of regret as I watched her retreat to the bed. "Willa, I'm sorry. I don't know what I'm feelin'."

She whirled around, her face a mask of fury. "You don't have to know what you're feeling. I only thought you should know. I mean, you were right. It only took one mishap."

I was probably the biggest bastard in the world for even thinking about wanting a baby when I wasn't even sure if I wanted a relationship yet, but I found myself in awe of this whole situation. It hit me out of nowhere and I didn't trust the feeling. Not yet. I needed to think about this and what her revelation meant long term. Then I'd figure out what I wanted to do about Willa in my life. "OK, honey."

"Don't call me honey! I'm not your honey! I'm not your *anything*!" With her small explosion of anger came two tears, which she wiped away with an angry swipe of her hand.

"I'm making this worse."

"You think?" she snarked.

I raised my hands in what I hoped was a non-threatening gesture. "It was a reflex, Willa. A chauvinistic one, but a reflex. I won't do it again."

"Good." She still looked supremely pissed, and I couldn't blame her. We stood there in silence for a moment, and I felt the heat of her glowering gaze burning into me. Finally, she turned away and walked over to the window.

"Look, I'm sorry." I scrubbed a hand over my face. The news had rocked me, but instead of draining

my energy as the adrenaline wore off, I found myself…
energized. "I'm not trying to be a jerk. I just don't
know what to say."

She sighed, her shoulders slumping slightly.
"Then don't say anything," she said. "Just let me be
mad for a while. Then maybe I can talk about this like
an adult." Willa took a few shaky breaths before
turning back around. The anger had melted away,
replaced with sadness and a sense of regret that
seemed to come from somewhere deep within her.
"I'm sorry. I have no right to be angry at you. I'm an
adult. I can deal with this."

"Sure, you can deal with this. You've got a core
of steel inside you just like your mother, but you don't
have to deal with this all on your own. I'm here to help
you. It's as much my mistake as it was yours."

She scowled again. "Mistake," she hissed. "You
want to know what my mistake was?" I opened my
mouth to answer but she plowed on. "My mistake was
being attracted to you in the first Goddamned place.
You're not worth my infatuation or attraction." She put
one hand over her stomach, like it was churning
uncomfortably. When she shoved past me and sprinted
for the bathroom, I realized I was right.

Willa vomited over and over, retching so hard it
made me wince. I ambled over to the bathroom to find
her leaning over the toilet, struggling to hold her hair
out of the way and stay upright at the same time.

Before I realized what I was doing, I found
myself gathering her hair to hold it back in a ponytail
at the back of her head before snaking an arm around
her middle to hold her up. If she noticed, she was too
sick to say anything.

It seemed like she was sick forever. Not
constantly but in waves. Between times, she'd sit back,

whimpering and spitting in the toilet every few seconds before flushing. A couple minutes later, it would start again. All the while, I stayed with her, murmuring nonsense to try to comfort her when I had no clue what to do. I knew one thing. We weren't leaving tomorrow. She needed rest and care before taking a four-hour trip back to what was likely going to be a very uncomfortable situation for her. Fuck. For both of us.

Eventually, she was done. She pulled away from me and lay down on the cool, tiled floor for a while. I stood and got a wet cloth and a glass of water before curling up on the floor beside her. I wiped her face gently until she looked up at me, taking the cloth from me to finish up. After she'd gotten her breath back, she sat up and rinsed her mouth before spitting in the toilet once more and flushing.

"Let's get you to bed," I said, trying to sound gentle.

She nodded, still pale and exhausted, but struggling to her feet. I stood as well, steadying her as we went into the bedroom. I wanted to pick her up and carry her, but I was afraid I'd shatter the fragile truce we had going on. I watched as she crawled onto the bed, lying on her side and curling up into a ball. Then I stood in the doorway for a few moments, debating whether or not to leave. When I heard a muffled sob, I knew there was no way I was leaving her alone.

With a sigh, I walked back to the bed and climbed in beside her. She allowed me to pull her into a loose embrace, burying her face in my chest. That's how we stayed, holding each other for a long time, until the sobs had stopped and her breathing evened out. Looking down at her, I could see the tear stains under her eyes and on her cheeks. She looked so lost and forlorn even as she slept it hurt my heart. When had this woman gotten so thoroughly under my skin?

Was it because I knew she was carrying my child? Or was it the woman herself? I was beginning to think it was a lot of both. Even if she chose to abort the child, I knew I'd never stop thinking about Willa. Mainly because there hadn't been an hour during the last six weeks when I hadn't thought about her.

With a sigh, I pulled the covers higher over her sleeping form. I wasn't sure what I was going to do or how much of an input she'd let me have in this situation, but I knew I wanted to be in her life and the baby's. Assuming she decided to keep the child.

Which brought up another dilemma. She was nineteen. I was thirty-five. The age gap wasn't insurmountable, but everyone was different. Just because her parents and mine had a similar age gap, as did several members of Bones and their old ladies, didn't mean she'd accept me even if I was interested in keeping her for my own. Which I wasn't. *I wasn't*!

Tomorrow. I'd figure it out tomorrow. Right now, I was tired and needed sleep. If I wasn't in top mental condition when she woke, there was no way I could hold my own with her. Especially not with the bombshell she'd dropped.

With that last thought, I settled her just that little bit closer, dropped a kiss on the top of her head, and closed my eyes. Soon after, sleep took me.

Chapter Seven
Willa

I woke up warm and cozy, a comforting, familiar scent surrounding me. It took me a couple of seconds to realize that Cyclone was in the bed with me and was wrapped around me in an intimate embrace. I glanced up to see his sleeping face, illuminated by the soft moonlight coming in from the window. His brows furrowed slightly, as if he was deep in thought, and I found myself wondering what he was dreaming about.

I was pulled out of my musing when the reason I'd woken up nudged me in the bladder. I knew it was impossible for me to feel the baby move at this point, but my bladder didn't care. I extracted myself from Cyclone's arms and padded to the bathroom. My whole body hurt. I probably hadn't moved since I'd fallen asleep.

Once I'd done my business, I washed my hands and brushed my teeth. Looking in the mirror, I studied my reflection for a long time. My eyes were bloodshot from my bout of sickness and crying, and there were dark circles under them. My cheekbones stood out sharply. It was a shock to see how my appearance had changed in only six weeks. I figured it was more from stress than the actual pregnancy itself, but I had started getting sick a week and a half ago and vomited most days at least once.

I splashed some cold water on my face and vowed to move on to the next step, whatever that was. I'd figure it out. The first thing I needed to do was to try and get some sleep. I'd need it in the morning when I headed back with Cyclone. With that thought, I turned to head back into the bedroom.

When I opened the door, I saw that Cyclone had

moved to the edge of the mattress and sat up. Waiting on me?

He cleared his throat. "Hey." He stood slowly, moving toward me. "I didn't want to bother you, so I stayed here. Thought you'd want some privacy." He looked back over his shoulder at the bed, waving a hand in that general direction. "Are you all right? Do you need anything?"

I nodded, but the tightness in my chest told a different story. I couldn't keep up the lie any longer. "No, Cyclone. I'm not okay. I haven't been since that night." My voice came out shaky, betraying my emotions. God, I was so done with crying! He wasn't worth crying over and I was just too exhausted to spend that much energy again.

Cyclone's expression shifted from concern to worry. "What can I do to help, Willa? That's all I want. To help. To make things better for you."

"Why are you here, Daniel?" It was the first time I'd called him by anything other than his road name except for when he'd answered the phone and I'd expected to talk to Bohannon.

He was silent for a long moment, and I thought maybe he wasn't going to tell me or that he would make up some bullshit reason. Instead, he scrubbed a hand through his hair and muttered his response. "I wish to God I fuckin' knew." Without looking at me, he held out a hand. "Come back to bed. We're not heading back in the morning because you need rest. There's no reason to hurry back, especially when we have stuff between us that needs to be resolved."

"I don't want to talk about it right now."

"I know. And I'm not sure I'm ready to talk either. There's so much rolling around in my mind and I need a chance to process it all."

"I know what you mean," I muttered. "I've had a few days to deal with it and I'm still not there."

"Then let's rest here and relax for a while. Tomorrow. The next day. Whatever it takes. Once we've both had time to come to terms with what's already happened, we'll figure out what's going to happen next. Together."

I wanted to deny him, but the truth was, he was right. Any decision I made, he deserved to be a part of, if he wanted to be. He hadn't asked for this any more than I had but done was done. He was also right that I'd had far longer to process being pregnant than he had.

"You're not stupid, Cyclone. You knew when I told you I was pregnant the baby was yours."

He gave a heavy sigh. Did I imagine the tinge of red that spread over his cheeks? "Yeah. I knew. Was hoping I was wrong, but I knew."

"Do you still wish you were wrong?" I hated how small I sounded, that his words affected me so much when he obviously didn't want to be in this situation. Also, that thought made me feel like a hypocrite because I didn't want to be pregnant either. But the fact was, I wouldn't want this baby to be anyone's other than Cyclone's.

He didn't answer immediately. Instead, he held my gaze for several moments, taking a couple of slow, deep breaths. "I can't answer that honestly, Willa. Give me some time to think. Like I said, we've got time. I have no intention of leaving here until we've both decided what we want to do. Can you give me that?"

I lowered my gaze. "Yeah. I can do that. I want any decision I make to be rational and I'm not capable of that right now."

Cyclone's hand enveloped mine as he led me

back to the bed. "Come on." He urged me to climb in first. I followed his direction, sliding under the sheets, feeling the cool softness of the material against my skin. He climbed in beside me, his body warm and welcoming as he pulled me back against him, spooning his body around mine.

God, I loved being in his arms. It had felt just as good that morning when I'd woken up so hung over. The longer we lay there quietly, the more the tension between us faded away to be replaced by a sense of comfort I hadn't felt before. In that moment, it felt like everything would be all right. Cyclone would help me. He'd make sure I had what I needed in material things and possibly even emotional support. We might not be in a relationship or be a couple, but I knew he'd do right by me. If not, my daddy and his momma would probably kill him. But that wasn't who Cyclone was. He wouldn't shirk his responsibilities for any reason. Which was another thing I worried about.

"I don't want you to try to forge some kind of relationship with me out of duty or obligation. You can be part of the baby's life if you want to be without us being a couple. The last thing I want to do is make you miserable."

"You won't, honey." There was a pause and he stiffened. "Sorry. Slipped out."

Try as I might, I couldn't suppress the giggle that escaped. "It's OK. I might have overreacted about the nickname. Just a touch."

"For what it's worth, it's an endearment I mean. You've always been sweet as honey as long as I've known you."

"I've had a crush on you since I was old enough to think boys weren't gross." I wasn't sure why I let that slip. It probably made me seem even more pathetic than I already did.

He sighed. "I'm sorry this happened, Willa. But I'd be a Goddamned liar if I told you the whole situation didn't affect me. I'm still working through my emotions, but I have a need to be close to you. Holding you... it soothes me somehow. I can't explain it any better. At least not yet."

That surprised me.

I snuggled deeper into Cyclone's warm embrace, feeling his heartbeat against my back. His words touched me deeply, and I could feel the emotions swirling inside me. It was a strange feeling, being so vulnerable with him. "It soothes me too." My voice was barely above a whisper, and I don't know if he heard me.

I have no idea why I decided to turn over to face Cyclone. I looked up into his face and found an intensity in his eyes that made my mouth go dry. My pulse quickened as I studied him. What was happening between us was more than just a comforting embrace and reassurance. It was a connection, a bond I couldn't explain and didn't want to think about right now. I was still angry at the man. At least, I knew I needed to be. As if magnetized, our lips met, and a spark ignited. And I was lost.

We kissed lightly at first, then he deepened the kiss and I followed willingly. Eagerly. Our bodies molded together as if they belonged to each other. The world melted away, leaving only the two of us lost in pleasure. Cyclone's hands moved down to my hips, pulling me even closer against him as we continued to kiss.

My mind was spinning, trying to understand what was happening and trying to decide if I wanted to push him away. I probably needed to, but did I really want to? No. I knew I didn't want him to stop. Cyclone ignited a fire inside me that I had no hope of getting under control. There was a sense of euphoria as I surrendered to the moment, my body entwined with his. He pulled back slightly to look at me, his eyes clouded with pleasure.

"I'm not sure what will happen tomorrow, but I want tonight. And it's not just about sex."

I blinked up at him, confused and lust stupid. "It's not?"

"I thought it was, baby, but my feelings are so far from 'just sex' it's not even funny."

"But… you don't want a woman." Confusion warred with hurt, and I put a little more distance between us. "If you don't want sex with me, just say so. It's not like I'd force myself on you." Did I sound bitter? Maybe. I did push back then, but his arms tightened around me, not letting me move away from him like I desperately needed to.

"I don't want a woman in my life. At least…" He shook his head, his brow furrowing. "I didn't. Now, I'm not so sure."

My heart beat so hard it was a roar in my ears. How many nights had I lain awake wishing he'd seek me out? Had I stopped wanting him after that disastrous morning after? No. I hadn't. I wasn't sure I'd ever stop wanting Cyclone. "I know you probably won't believe me considering I came to that party for one reason, but I don't think I can do casual sex again. You were… I mean… I hadn't ever…"

"I know." He smiled tenderly at me, stroking my cheek with the pad of his thumb. "At least, I figured. There was blood on the sheets. I was your first lover. Wasn't I?" Then he stilled, his eyes narrowing. "Why did you come to that party?"

I snorted. "To get laid. That's why I'd started drinking. To keep my courage up."

"So, any of my brothers would have done?" The emotions on his face changed so rapidly it was hard to keep up. But I thought I saw anger, bitterness... maybe even a touch of hurt.

"No. I meant it when I said I'd had a crush on you for a long time. While I admit I wasn't sure whose lap I fell into, my intention was always to try to seduce you."

Trembling in his arms, I whimpered. I'd laid myself bare to him. He knew how long I'd wanted him. He knew he'd taken my virginity. And he was still in bed with me, about to make love to me again. Or, rather, he was about to have sex with me again. At least, I kind of hoped that's what we were going to do.

"So it was me."

"Yes, Daniel. It's always been you." My voice was barely above a whisper. I knew it was a bad idea, that it probably made me too stupid to live, but I wanted this one last time. We might never do this again, might never share all this passion I thought might affect both of us, but I wanted it. One time. Sober so I could enjoy it fully.

He stroked my cheek, giving me a gentle smile before leaning in to kiss my lips softly. When he pulled back, he pressed his forehead to mine. "Then, let's do it right this time. We're both stone-cold sober. We both know I've already gotten you pregnant. There's an attraction between us I can't fight and I ain't even sure I want to try."

"Cyclone..."

"Shh..." He kissed me again before continuing. "I ain't promisin' a happily ever after, but I'd like to at least explore what it's like to have you in my life, Willa.

If it doesn't work out, at least we'll know."

"One day at a time?"

"That's it exactly." I bit my lip, glancing away from him, but Cyclone caught my chin gently and turned my face back up to his. "I promise I won't betray you, honey. I won't slip behind your back and fuck other women. While we're working this out, it's me and you. No one else. If either of us decide it's not right, we'll talk to the other about it before we move on. Yes?"

That sounded better. "You promise?"

"I do. And I never break my word. It's something Cain taught me almost from the moment me and Cliff came to live at Bones. I'm not perfect, as evidenced by the way I've handled this situation so far, but I never break my word."

I nodded my head. "Then yes. I'd like to see what happens next."

He grinned before leaning into me, pressing his lips to mine once more. Nothing had ever felt more right. Now that we'd come up with a plan -- even if it was to wait on making any decisions -- I felt better.

I'd admitted to having feelings for him. Well, at least as much as he'd admitted to feeling something for me. For a man like Cyclone to tell me he was confused about his feelings, to admit he didn't know what he needed to do was oddly reassuring. No matter how much I wished he was so madly in love with me he'd embrace having the child we'd conceived, I was glad he was taking his time to work through all the angles. The last thing I wanted was for either of us to rush into something. No matter how much I truly wanted it. I absolutely would not be miserable because I'd chased a dream.

With a sigh, I surrendered to Cyclone. His kisses

were sweet and hot. I loved the way he made me feel. Like I was the most important person in his world. The way he held me so carefully, stroking my back with one hand while he cradled my head with the other.

His tongue swept into my mouth, stroking in an erotic slide. It took minutes of his drugging kisses before I was a whimpering, moaning, needy mass of nerve endings. Had it been this good the last time? And this was only his kiss!

"I want you," I whimpered as he pulled back. I didn't want him to stop. Not now. Maybe not ever.

"Good," he murmured. "Because I want you too."

His mouth found mine again, deepening the kiss until I was clinging to him. My arms circled his neck, my hands were buried in his hair. His body moved against mine, and I reveled in the feel of his hard muscles and every inch of hot skin that pressed against mine.

Cyclone groaned against my lips, and his hands slid up my side to cup one breast. I gasped, arching my back into his touch.

"You're driving me crazy," he murmured against my mouth. "You taste so fuckin' sweet."

"It's a two-way street," I mumbled, needing to get closer to him. I needed to get my clothes off so he could caress my skin.

It felt like everything faded away and it was just the two of us. For those few moments, we were suspended in time, connected and intertwined with no worries other than exploring each other.

I was lost in the sensations of his hands, his mouth, his body against mine. Every movement caused a wave of pleasure to spread throughout my body. I felt myself melting with each touch, growing more and more addicted to him.

When Cyclone moved off me, pushing himself up on stiffened arms, I whimpered in protest.

"Shh, honey. I'm not going anywhere." He used one hand to reach back between his shoulder blades and strip off his shirt. Tattooed muscles rippled with every movement. Brawny arms, defined chest, and ripped abs seemed to dance before my avid gaze.

"Daniel…" I breathed his name like a prayer. And maybe it was. "Please don't break my heart." The words slipped out before I could censor them. Even as I pleaded with him, I knew he was destined to do just that. This man would break my heart because Cyclone was a force of nature, not someone to be controlled. No matter what he thought now, he'd grow to see me and any child I carried as trying to control him. Even knowing that, I still wanted this time together. I wanted to remember every blistering second of what we were about to share.

"Trust me, Willa," he said as he gently removed my sleep shirt. "One day at a time. One moment at a time. We'll get through tonight together. Then we'll take on tomorrow. Then the next day. OK? One day at a time."

I nodded and let my hands find his chest. I caressed the skin beneath my palms up to his shoulders and down his muscled arms.

Then he lowered his head to my breast, and I cried out when his lips closed over one nipple. He pulled gently, sucking first one peak then the other. Whenever he switched sides, his fingers toyed with my flesh until I was crying out and writhing beneath him.

"Such sweet nipples," he rasped against my skin. "Could suck on these forever."

"Oh, God!" I cried as he sucked me harder,

stretching my nipple until it slipped from his mouth with an audible pop.

"Need more." Cyclone's needy growl was an aphrodisiac.

He trailed his mouth down my torso to just above my mound. Had he done this last time? I thought he had. My breath came in sharp pants and my body was coated in a fine sheen of sweat. I was lightheaded and my pussy tingled with excitement. Then his mouth closed over my clitoris, and I was lost.

Holding my thighs apart, Cyclone licked and sucked at my lips, growling against my wet folds as he dragged his tongue from pussy to clit over and over again. Every touch of his mouth and every stroke of his fingers had me on edge. When he finally plunged two fingers inside me, I came in a hard, wet rush, screaming his name.

I was lost in the sensations of his hands and his mouth on my body. Every movement caused a wave of pleasure to spread throughout my body. I felt myself melting with each touch, growing more and more addicted to him.

When Cyclone finally drew away, I felt like I'd been deprived of something vital. But he only crawled up my body, kissing me once again. I tasted myself on his lips and tongue, but it only inflamed me further.

He sat up on his knees to shove his sleep pants from his hips. When he did, his cock bobbed proudly from a dark thatch of curls beneath that hard Adonis belt. He was, in a word, mesmerizing.

"You're so beautiful," I murmured, reaching out to stroke the length of him.

He groaned and closed his eyes, enjoying my touch. I let my fingers travel up and down slowly before grasping his base and stroking up slowly. I had a vague recollection of touching him like this before. Of stroking his cock until he batted my hand away and sank into my pussy. Would he do it again?

Cyclone hissed out a breath before grabbing my wrist. "Stop," he murmured. "You're driving me fuckin' crazy, woman."

He leaned down and kissed me deeply before shifting his hips back. Then he pushed forward into my wet pussy. I gasped as he filled me, eyes wide and lips parted as pleasure unlike anything I could remember before washed over me.

His thrusts were slow and steady as his gaze held mine captive. He seemed to be gauging my every reaction, looking for… something.

Cyclone growled in pleasure and then grabbed my wrists and pinned them to the bed as he lay fully on top of me. His eyes glinted with a feral intensity that sent a thrill of anticipation through my body. This wasn't a man unaffected by what we were doing. He was deeply affected. It might have been only lust, but he wasn't as in control as I'd have thought he would be. I wouldn't say I was at all torn up about it either. I loved this intensity, the way his gaze ate me up.

He increased his thrusts, pushing deeper -- my breath caught in my throat as I felt the orgasm building inside me. I wanted to be in this moment forever, a part of this wildness that consumed us both. When I couldn't take it any longer, I cried out, my hips bucking wildly as I came with a brutal intensity. My pussy clamped down on him, and Cyclone let out his own deep shout of completion. Hot cum filled me and I welcomed the sensation, letting the pleasure wash over me as it would. Another powerful orgasm rocked me, and I cried out his name as I clung to him as tightly as I could with arms and legs.

When it was over, when we'd both relaxed somewhat, I was still panting, trying to catch my breath. It was the most wonderful experience of my life. I couldn't help but wonder if he'd repeat it before we left for Kentucky.

Cyclone pulled away from me and rested his forehead against mine, his breathing still labored. "You," he said quietly. "Your body was made to be pleasured."

He looked into my eyes and smiled before pressing a soft kiss to my lips. I smiled back, feeling my cheeks heat up as I wrestled with the urge to hold him to me. I didn't want this to end. Not yet.

With one final kiss, Cyclone pushed himself off me and slid from the bed. "I'll be right back, baby. Don't get up."

He stalked to the bathroom. I heard water running, then he returned with a cloth. I tried to close my legs, but he gently pushed them apart before cleaning my pussy. I blushed. The act was too intimate. Almost like he really cared about me.

Then he tossed the cloth back in the direction of the bathroom and climbed back into bed with me. Pulling me close, he tilted my chin up for another, gentle kiss.

"Get some rest. We'll get breakfast in the morning, then talk." He smiled down at me. "You good?"

"You seem to always be asking me that same question."

He chuckled. "Yeah, I guess I do."

"But yes. I think I am good."

"Honey, you're better than good. You're absolutely fuckin' perfect."

Chapter Eight

Cyclone

When I woke up, I had a satisfying feeling of *déjà vu*. My head was resting on the most perfect set of tits I'd ever had the pleasure of lying on, with one pert nipple right in front of my face. Naturally, I shifted just that little bit so I could lave it with my tongue.

Willa moaned in her sleep. I glanced up at the peaceful look on her face. One small hand was tunneled in my hair. When I flicked her nipple again, her fingers flexed and she moaned louder, this time arching her back slightly. I couldn't help but grin.

I'd fucked her several times over the hours we'd been in bed. Each time I took her, I wanted more. The pleasure was indescribable.

OK, no. I didn't fuck her. What I did with Willa this time wasn't fucking. That was what we'd done the first night. This was… If I had to put a name on it, I'd say it was making love. Thanks to Cain and Angel, I'd been able to learn what love was and how it felt, but this was different. Not only did I have this all-consuming need to make everything right in Willa's world, but there was a protective possession to my feelings. I wanted her with me and only me. Any other motherfucker who even looked at her would feel my wrath.

I pulled back from her nipple and lay there smiling. Willa stirred again and started to wake up. I leaned up and kissed her sweet lips before whispering in her ear, "Good morning, beautiful." That was when I heard it. She laughed, like the tinkling of a bell.

Her lips lifted and her deep brown eyes were heavy-lidded with pleasure as her lips stayed curled in happiness. "Good morning, Cyclone." I pulled her closer and kissed her, long and deep with a tenderness I'd never shown a woman. Had never wanted to show a woman.

We lay like that for a while, tangled together. I felt more content than I ever had before, and I realized it was all Willa. I'd never felt so alive, and I never wanted this closeness I'd found with her sometime in the night to end.

I'm not sure when those feelings built inside me, but something had clicked during the night when we'd made love. I was still struggling to figure out what those emotions all meant, but I knew I had to explore them with her. Only her. The thought of doing what I'd done with Willa through the night and into the wee hours of the morning with anyone else was a hard no. Something inside me had shifted. And I wasn't sure what to do about it.

"You want a shower?" I stroked her hair, still laying half on top of her and not in any hurry to move.

She bit her lip, looking unsure of herself. When she met my gaze again, she had a shy, almost pleading look on her face. "Will you come with me?"

I barked out a laugh. I wasn't sure what I expected her response to be but that wasn't it. "Thought you'd want some privacy, but I'm all for running my soapy hands over your body."

That got a giggle from her. Given the glorious, eager smile she gave me, I knew I'd said the exact right thing.

She pushed at me, and I moved off her, so she could get out of the bed. "That sounds perfect."

Willa led the way, for which I would be eternally grateful. The woman had an ass to make angels weep.

I adjusted the water and let her step in ahead of me. When I stepped in behind her, she slid into my arms like we'd done this a thousand times. She put her arms around my neck and pressed against me like she was starved for my touch. I wasn't altogether sure I wasn't starved for hers.

"Cyclone," was all she said, but it was filled with so much desire it made my heart skip a beat.

My heated gaze dropped to her lips, and I kissed her like I'd found my home in her. Like I'd never want to stop. And the thing was, I might not ever want to. And I wasn't altogether sure how I felt about needing her this much.

I bent my head and kissed her. Not a sensual, sexy kiss, but a deep, abiding one that spoke of all the emotions I was feeling. I kissed her long and slow in an effort to make her understand how deeply I was in. How deeply we were in. Because I sure as hell wasn't the only one feeling this shit. Willa wasn't *all* in and I didn't blame her. After the way I'd treated her, not just the past six weeks by ignoring her, for not checking on her, but for the way I started out when she first called.

Pulling back, I pressed my forehead against hers. I needed a moment to process my thoughts. We'd said we'd talk today but I wasn't sure I was ready. I mean, how did I tell her I was falling for her when I wasn't even sure I could admit it to myself?

"I'm sorry, Willa."

She froze, stiffening in my arms. I didn't let her go, but did reach for the shower gel with one hand. I squirted a stream over her breasts. Setting the bottle back on the shelf, I used the same hand to rub the gel into a gentle lather.

"Sorry? For what?"

"For the way I treated you. From that very first night."

"What?" She looked up at me, her eyes wide,

shocked.

"I've fucked things up with you from the first Goddamned moment you fell into my lap. And I'm so fuckin' sorry."

She gave a little shake of her head. I pulled her closer so her soapy breasts were mashed against my chest. I continued to rub my hands over her skin, this time down her back all the way to that pert ass of hers. "I don't under-- understand." Her voice broke, tears gathering in her lovely eyes.

"Honey, I should never have taken advantage of you that night. Being drunk was no excuse. You were drunk too, and I'm not sure you would have made the same choices if you hadn't been.

"Daniel, I got drunk so I could get up enough courage to have sex with someone." She frowned, then shook her head, lowering her gaze to my chest as if thinking through what she wanted to say. "No, that's not exactly right. I wanted it to be you." She looked up into my eyes again. "I'd hoped it would be you, but had no expectation you'd have me."

"If I'd been sober, I wouldn't have."

She winced and tried to push away. "Gee, Cyclone. Tell me how you really feel."

"Stop fighting me, Willa," I commanded gently. "Let me finish."

"Is this really the best time to talk? I mean, I feel a little too exposed. You know. Because I'm naked." Her temper was starting to spark again. And I'd be Goddamned if my cock, the fucking prick, didn't respond.

I chuckled. "Yeah, baby. I think this is the perfect time. This way, you can't get away from me."

She glared up at me. "You just said you didn't want me! What the fuck, Cyclone?"

"No. That's not what I said. I said I wouldn't have taken you to bed if I'd been sober." I knew I was grinning, and I was probably a crazy bastard, but I loved it when she got snippy with me.

"It's the same thing!" She shoved at me harder, seriously trying to get away this time. "Let me go, asshole!"

"Shh… calm down and let me finish. Do you seriously think I'd have taken you to bed, with you drunk off your ass, knowing who the fuck your daddy is if I'd been in my right mind?" I raised an eyebrow at her. She stilled and looked wary as if sensing a trap. "Never thought there was enough alcohol in the fuckin' world to make me do what I did with you that night. No. What I should have done was ask your father's permission to make you my old lady."

"Old lady? You never even noticed me. Not as anything other than a child."

"Oh, I noticed you, all right. Though, I admit, I never expected to have you in my bed." I backed her up so the spray hit her back, rinsing her with gentle strokes of my hands under the water. Then I turned her around and did the same to her front, cupping her tits as I did. Despite her ire, she moaned as I gently squeezed the slight mounds.

She let her head fall back to rest on my shoulder and I circled her small body with my arms, resting my mouth at her neck. I bit down gently, and she squealed.

"What I'm trying to say here," I spoke against her throat, inhaling the sweet scent of herbal soap and delicious woman, "is that I shouldn't have taken your virginity when we were both drunk and unable to make rational decisions. Not taken you to bed like an animal. The next question is, if we hadn't both been shit-faced, would I have made a move on you? The answer to that is probably not." Again, she stiffened but I plowed on. "But, now that it's done, we're gonna get to know each other. Just like we discussed last night. I'm gonna talk to your daddy and take my punishment like a man. After that, assuming he lets me live, we'll see if we can stand each other long enough to form a relationship." I kissed her shoulder before sliding my hand down to cup her pussy. "You with me?"

She shivered and made an affirmative sound. We both stood there, barely moving as the warm water ran down our bodies. I squeezed her once before turning her in my arms so she was facing me once again.

I urged her to lift her leg to hook over my hip and with one smooth thrust, I slid inside her.

Willa gasped, her eyes going wide before she whimpered and clutched at my shoulders. "Daniel! Oh, God!"

"Come, honey. Do it now!"

She screamed, clamping down on my cock as I thrust in and out of her. Her orgasm wanted to trigger my own, but I wasn't ready yet.

I pulled out, spinning her around and mashing her up against the shower wall, lifting her leg to place it on the low bench. One arm around her waist, the other at her hip, I shoved back inside her, caging her in with my body.

Willa shuddered against me, crying out in surprise when I started to move. I couldn't seem to get close enough to her. Couldn't get deep enough. Couldn't get… enough!

"Fuck… Fuck!"

I slammed into her as she bucked and tried to push back, meeting me thrust for thrust. Our mingled cries and grunts filled the bathroom as I finally surrendered to her sweet body.

With a brutal shout, I came deep inside her. Willa came with me, her body milking mine for all I had to give her. When it was over, her legs gave out and she sagged back against me. I knew how she felt. My own legs felt like jelly.

With shaking hands, I managed to get the water turned off before slumping on the bench with Willa in my arms. We were both breathing heavily. My heart pounded in my ears.

I reached for a towel on the rack beside the shower, drying first her, then me. "Come on, honey. Let's get dressed, then figure out where the fuck we're gonna go from here."

"All right." She looked up at me with something I hadn't thought I'd see, especially not this soon. Complete trust.

As I gazed into the fathomless dark pools of her eyes, I knew without a doubt she had me. I was well and truly fucked. Because there was no fucking way I would let Willa go. She was mine.

It was time I started acting like it.

Chapter Nine

Willa

After we showered -- and made love -- we dressed and went to breakfast. He took me to a little diner that had the best pancakes I'd ever eaten. I'm pretty sure the sounds I made as I ate were embarrassing, but Cyclone only grinned.

"Someone was hungry." He had a smug look on his face, like he'd accomplished a monumental task.

I shrugged. "What can I say? When it's good, it's good."

That got a bark of laughter out of him. His eyes crinkled at the corners, and I couldn't help but smile in return. I hadn't ever seen him look so relaxed before. I hadn't ever seen him look so carefree before.

Not even in bed.

We talked over breakfast, about nothing of consequence really, but it was nice. It felt… right. Like we belonged together.

When breakfast was done, Cyclone stood and dropped some bills on the table to settle the tab. Then he pulled me to my feet. "Come on, sunshine. We've got things to discuss."

I tried not to let the dread in my heart show, but when he peered down into my eyes, there was no way to keep my feelings from him. He gave me a tender smile, then pulled me to him for a brief hug before dropping a kiss on top of my head.

"Don't look so scared. We're gonna be fine."

"We?"

He took my hand and led me to the parking lot and the truck he'd brought to pick me up. I wished he'd brought his bike, but the weather was a little more than I was prepared for. Christmas was in less than a week and things had gone from unseasonably warm to very chilly overnight.

"Yeah. We. Thought we'd already decided we were giving this a shot."

"Oh. Well, OK." I know I sounded young and childish, but I was so nervous I didn't know what to say. And I was getting ready to have a very real adult conversation with a man I was equal parts terrified of and infatuated with.

He opened the door for me, and I climbed in. Once I'd fastened my seat belt, he shut the door and trotted around to his side. When he climbed in beside me, he reached over, finding my hand and giving it a firm, reassuring squeeze.

"Don't look so scared. I'll only take a bite out of you if you ask."

I couldn't help the way my body reacted to his words. I shivered and actually broke out into a sweat, gasping as my gaze jerked to his. He grinned and winked at me before starting the truck and heading back to the hotel.

As he opened the door to our suite, my phone chimed. I glanced at the screen to see my mother's name, requesting a FaceTime. I groaned. I wasn't sure I was ready to talk to her, but she'd be getting anxious and I didn't want her to worry more than she already was.

"Go," Cyclone said, urging me to the bedroom. "Talk with your mother."

"I don't know what to say." I felt like a little kid who knew she was in trouble and was avoiding her parents for as long as possible.

He shrugged those brawny shoulders and gave me a reassuring smile. "Tell her whatever you want. Better to prepare her for us coming home. You do that.

I'll call Trucker and we'll get this part of it over with."

And just like that, all those pancakes I'd eaten threatened to come up. "Oh, God. NO! Do not call my father." The phone had stopped chiming, but I knew my mother would call back in a few seconds. She always tried at least twice, knowing I was forever losing my phone.

Pulling me into his arms, Cyclone hugged me fiercely. "Honey, I have to. If he finds this out from anyone else, the ass beatin' I'd get wouldn't be just epic, it'd be catastrophic. Besides, I respect your father, though he's not going to believe that when I tell him everything. By avoiding you all this time, I earned every single thing he'll do to me when we get back. No matter if you want me long-term or not. I'm gonna be lucky to get out of this with my balls intact as it is." He tilted my chin up with gentle fingers and kissed me briefly. "You talk with your mom. Let her know you're good. Tell her everything. It will help you figure out how you really feel and what you want to say to me once these conversations are over. Because we still have things to settle between us."

I took a deep breath. "OK. It's just… I don't want to disappoint my mom." I couldn't help the tears that dripped from my eyes down my cheeks.

"Honey, she's your mother. She loves you more than life itself. She may not like some of the choices you make, but she would never be disappointed in you."

As I stared up at him, trying to find the reassurance I needed, my phone started chiming again. Cyclone framed my face with his hands and kissed me once again before giving me an encouraging smile and moving to the other side of the suite and shutting the connecting door.

I took a deep breath and answered the FaceTime call. "Hi, Mom." I gave her a bright smile, hoping like hell she thought I was happy to hear from her.

"Hi, sweetie. You hanging in there?"

"Yeah. I'm doing fine. Just contemplating how much weight my right foot needs to lose to keep this from happening again." I tried to make a joke but had to stifle the wince.

"Cruise control will become your new best friend, huh?" She still smiled, but I could tell she was still worried.

There was an awkward silence between us that I'd never experienced with my mother. She'd always been a mother and best friend all in one. I told her everything in my life. Always had. Any time I'd ever had a problem, Mom was the first person I ran to.

"Baby, what's going on? I know something's not right. I can't help you if I don't know what's happened."

"Mom, I'm pregnant."

She blinked several times then gave me a gentle smile. "I assume you didn't plan on this?"

"No." My reply was soft, and I looked away from the phone.

"It happens. Happened to me with you. Surely you know I'd never judge you or be angry at you for this. Right? I mean, I can hardly be angry when I was in a similar situation."

"I know. I'm sorry."

"Honey. Why are you sorry?" She sounded almost relieved. Had she been that worried about me? So worried that finding out her daughter was pregnant wasn't something she was angry about? "Things happen. While I wish you'd taken more precautions, this isn't the end of the world. Your father and I will help you in any way we can. If that's taking you to terminate the pregnancy, we will. If that means we help you raise the child, we'll be on board with that too. Baby. We love you! With all our hearts."

And yeah, the fucking tears started again, no matter how hard I tried to hold them back. "I'm so sorry, Mom. I didn't mean to shut you out. I just didn't know what to do."

She tilted her head, studying me for a long moment. "There's more. Isn't there?"

Right. How to answer that. If Cyclone was on the phone with Dad, then there was no reason not to tell my mother. Besides, if anyone could keep my dad from killing Cyclone, it was my mother. "Yeah. There's more." I chuckled as I used a tissue to wipe my nose. "A lot more."

"I'm guessing you need to start by telling me who the father is." She phrased it carefully and kept her tone as gentle as possible, but my mother knew me well enough to know the subject of the baby's father was the part she dreaded the most.

"Yeah." I shook my head once, not believing I was having this conversation and really not wanting to divulge this, but it had to be done. "Cyclone. Daniel Gill is the father."

My mother's expression didn't change. She still had a mild, pleasant look on her face, but something in her eyes told me she was considering all the possibilities and not liking the outcome of any of them. "I see. I suppose that's why he insisted on coming after you himself?"

"He didn't know until he got here. I only found out myself a few days before I left."

"Did he... hurt you, honey?"

"What? NO! He'd never hurt me, Mom. I mean,

yeah, he was an asshole at first, but not in a mean kind of way. Just a clueless, *guy* kind of way."

My mom pursed her lips and I thought she might be trying to hold back a grin at my description.

"Yeah, I could see that. Most men tend to be that way sometimes."

"It didn't help that I didn't cushion the blow. I just… blurted it out."

That did get a laugh from her. And just like that, the tension inside me eased. I had to tell her the rest because I knew Cyclone would tell Dad and my father would need my mother to keep him from killing Cyclone.

"There's more, Mom."

"Oh?"

"Yeah. We were both at the party a few weeks ago. That's when it happened."

Her gaze turned speculative, and I knew she'd work it out before I had the chance to tell her. "Were you --" She cleared her throat. "Were you drunk, Willa?"

"Yeah. I was. But before you go assuming the worst, he was too. And I got drunk on purpose." I said it all in a rush, needing to stop the murderous thoughts I could practically see running through her mind.

"You got drunk on purpose." It wasn't a question. More like she wasn't quite sure she could believe I'd done something that stupid.

"Yes." I took in a deep breath before letting it out. "I wanted to have sex. You know. For the first time. I did it at the club because I knew the men there would be safe, but also because I kind of hoped it would be Cyclone."

Her expression softened, but just as quickly turned stern. "You know you've put your father in a pretty bad position. He's not going to like this at all."

"Yes. I know. I didn't quite think that part all the way through."

"Have the two of you talked about this?"

"Yes. Well, somewhat. Just enough to know we want to try being together. Assuming Dad doesn't kill him first." I muttered that last part, saying it more to myself than my mother.

"That's a very big 'if,' sweetie." She shook her head just as I heard a very loud, very angry roar in the background.

"What do you fuckin' mean you got my daughter pregnant?"

My mother winced. "Yeah. A very big 'if'."

"Mom, please help me." The tears were threatening again. "I think I might love him."

"Honey, I know you love him. At least, you love the idea of him. You have since you were ten."

My eyes widened. "You knew about that?"

"You're my daughter. A mother notices things." She gave me a knowing nod. Then there was more shouting in the background.

"You get your fuckin' bitch ass back to this clubhouse with my daughter, you bastard! When you do, you better have made your peace with Jesus because the prospects will have your fuckin' grave dug by the time you get back. We'll have a nice little ceremony right after I piss on your fuckin' headstone!"

"Yeah." I shivered, tears flowing freely now. "A very big 'if'."

Chapter Ten

Cyclone

"You get your fuckin' bitch ass back to this clubhouse with my daughter, you bastard! When you do, you better have made your peace with Jesus because the prospects will have your fuckin' grave dug by the time you get back. We'll have a nice little ceremony right after I piss on your fuckin' headstone!"

To say Trucker was pissed as shit didn't even come close to what the man was feeling. The odds of my surviving this dropped from near zero to less than zero. Didn't matter. I wasn't giving Willa up. If that meant I lived out the rest of my life nutless and drinking my food through a straw, I'd take it. Of course, it kind of sounded like he didn't plan on letting me live that long. Before I could say anything more, he disconnected the call.

"Well. That could have gone better." I scrubbed a hand over my face before laying my phone on the table and moving to the connecting door. I was about to knock when Willa opened the door and looked up at me. There were tears on her cheeks and a wave of fury washed through me.

She gasped and took a step back. Yeah. I needed to rein it in. Again. Seemed to be my motto of late. "Sorry, honey. Didn't expect your mother would make you cry. Doesn't seem like her."

"She didn't. But I heard my dad in the background." As she spoke, more tears spilled over. "He's not going to let us be together." Then she dissolved into more tears.

I pulled her into my arms, lifting her so I could carry her to the couch. She straddled my hips and wrapped her arms around my neck, clinging to me as I rubbed my hands up and down her back. "It's all going to be fine. I promise you, Willa. We'll get through this."

"I'm so sorry, Daniel. So sorry."

"You've got nothing to be sorry for. I never do anything I don't want to do."

"But I practically targeted you! Sure, stumbling onto you outside the clubhouse was an accident, but I came there hoping it would be you."

"You want to know a secret?" I couldn't believe I was about to tell her this, but she needed to hear it. "After talking with Trucker, hearing his rather vocal and violent pushback, instead of feeling relieved I wouldn't have to take on a woman, that I'd be getting that beating I so richly deserved before I went on my merry way, I found myself pushing back just as hard as he did. Not aggressively. That ain't the way to handle a man as big as Trucker. But I'd told him in no uncertain terms that if you'd have me, I was keeping you. Whether or not he approved." Her eyes got wider and wider as I spoke. "And I meant every fuckin' word, honey."

"Daniel?" There was a becoming blush staining her cheeks and she trembled in my arms. Her eyes were wide and glassy as tears still dripped from them.

"I noticed you, Willa. At the compound. Yeah, I watched you grow up, but I noticed you as a woman. I tried to block it out, to deny I noticed because you were as off-limits as it got. But I saw you. When you fell in my lap that night, I think on some level I knew it was you. I mean, there was no way I was in a state to think rationally, but I knew you were familiar to me. I didn't look too closely at who you were because I wanted you with every part of my fuckin' being."

"And now?" Her voice was soft, vulnerable.

"The only way I'm letting you get away from me

is if you tell me you don't want me. I'll always respect your wishes, but even then, I'd be lying if I said I'd let you leave without a fight. I want you, Willa. You and this baby. So, the ball's in your corner."

"Oh, Daniel!" She threw her arms around my neck again, and the tears came in racking sobs into my neck.

"Don't cry, honey. Please. I can't stand for you to be sad."

"I'm not," she said, her voice muffled by my neck. "I'm just so…"

"Relieved?"

"Yes! I didn't think you wanted a woman. You even said so. I said it before, but I don't want you with me out of a sense of obligation."

"I never do anything I don't want to do. Even taking the vice presidency of Bones. Sure, Cain forced me into it, but I'd have told him to pick someone else if I really hadn't wanted to do it. It's a burden sometimes, and I'm still learning, but if my dad needs me to do something, then I give it a good effort. So, I might not have chosen the situation -- with you or with Bones -- but I'm all in. With both. Though, I gotta tell you. I think I'm gonna be happier with you than I am with being vice president of Bones. And I'm pretty fuckin' happy with being vice president."

She sat back on my lap, swiping her eyes with the sleeve of her shirt. "So, you'll take me on? Make me your old lady?"

"Oh yeah, honey. It'll be rough goin' with Trucker, but I'll prove to him and Helen that I can be what you need. We might not love each other yet, but there is a mutual respect that will grow. And to be honest?" I waited until I had her undivided attention, her gaze focused squarely on mine. "I think I'm more than halfway in love with you all ready."

The smile she gave me was brilliant, if still a bit tearful. But I could see she believed me. What I didn't tell her, and what I wasn't sure I was fully prepared to admit even to myself, was that I was already way the fuck past halfway in love with her.

We stayed the night in Waynesville, talking. Making love. How the fuck had I managed to live this long without having this kind of closeness with another person? I finally got it. Spending a night fucking a club girl wasn't nearly as satisfying as making love with my woman.

I got Kickstand to make arrangements to have Willa's car brought back to Bones, and Willa was finishing packing up her shit when my phone rang.

I glanced at the screen and winced. Ice. My brother as well as my president.

"You calling as Cliff or Ice?" I didn't bother with formalities. Cliff would understand.

"Both, you dumbass. What the fuck did you do to Trucker's daughter? And don't tell me it ain't none of my business because, A: I'm the president of Bones MC, and B: I'm your fuckin' brother. Right now, from the sound of it, you're gonna need both solidly in your corner."

"Congratulations," I said dryly. "You're gonna be an uncle."

Ice chuckled. "Yeah. Good one. Tell me what's really going on." When I didn't say anything his laughter died down. "You're serious, aren't you." It wasn't a question.

"You think I'd joke about that? With Trucker's daughter? I might be an asshole, but I'm not a stupid asshole." Yeah. The irony wasn't lost on me.

"So actually knocking up the daughter of a man

as big as Trucker is better than joking about knocking her up. Yeah. Not stupid at all, Cyclone." If my brother's tone of voice was any indication he was nearly as angry with me as Trucker was.

"It is what it is, brother. She's agreed to be my old lady, so I'm not really sure what the problem is. Ain't sayin' we're in love, but we'll get there."

"You know he's callin' for your patch, right? Not only does he want you replaced as vice president, but he wants you out of Bones." Where there had been background noise before, I heard a door close, and all the chatter died down. "He said you took advantage of her when she was drunk. That's rape, Cyclone. Pure and simple. Not only will that cost you your patch, Trucker would have every right to fuckin' kill you, and no one in this entire Goddamned compound would lift a fuckin' finger to help you. Even Dad can't get you out of that."

"Trust me when I say he'd have every right and I wouldn't even try to defend myself."

"You're Goddamned right he would! What the fuck, Dan? What the Goddamned fuck?"

"Daniel? Is everything OK?" Willa had walked in on the conversation and no doubt had heard my brother yelling at me.

"Yeah, honey. It's all good."

"No, it's not." She moved to my side. "I could hear someone all the way in the next room. Is that my dad again?"

"Nah. It's my brother."

"Ice? Why is he yelling?"

I sighed. I didn't want her involved in this conversation. "It's nothing. Let me wrap this up and we'll get on the road.

As if I'd flipped a switch, Willa's face hardened

instantly. She held out her hand. "Give me the phone."

I raised an eyebrow at her. "Much as I appreciate you being upset on my behalf, I'm not givin' you the phone, honey. I'll deal with my brother or your father or anyone else I have to. Not you."

As if I hadn't just told her no, Willa moved to my side and plucked the phone right outta my fucking hand. With a glare up at me, she put the phone on speaker.

"Ice. This is Willa."

There was a pause before Ice said anything. "I need to talk to my brother alone, Willa. I'm sorry, but this is club business."

"Seems like it's about me, which makes me club business, which means I will have my say. Now what's the fucking problem?" Oh, that little snippy voice of hers was gonna get her fucked but good. For some odd reason, that particular tone of voice made my cock hard as granite when I knew I shouldn't encourage her. Any other woman I'd have put in her place, but Willa was right where she needed to be. The old lady of an MC VP.

Again, there was silence before Ice continued. "Uh --" He coughed once. "-- I need to, uh, ask you if --" He cleared his throat. "Well, did Cyclone, uh, you know, take advantage of you when you, uh --" Another throat clear. "I mean, were you drunk when the two of you..." If this had been any other situation I'd be laughing my ass off. Still might. I'd bring this up over and over at family Christmas dinners. It'd be a hoot.

"You mean, did he fuck me without my consent? No. In fact, if anyone took advantage of anyone in that situation it was me. He was so drunk I'm not sure he knew where he was exactly, let alone who I was."

When Ice didn't say anything -- I really wish he'd FaceTimed us because I'd love to see his expression -- she continued. "I set out at that party to lose my virginity. I had Cyclone in mind, though I'd never have been brave enough to approach him without some liquid courage. So? I got drunk. Landed in his lap. And things took a natural progression. And you know what? It was absolutely *glorious*."

After another brief pause, Ice continued in a cheerful voice. "OK, then. 'Nuff said." A chuckle I was sure my brother hadn't meant to let loose sounded over the speaker before he cleared his throat again. "You kids have fun. See you when you get home." Then he ended the call.

Willa looked up at me, all sweet and innocent. "Was it something I said?"

Chapter Eleven

The trip to the compound was enjoyable. More than enjoyable. I'm not certain I've laughed so hard in my entire life. Cyclone and I got to know each other in the four hours it took to get home.

He was actually a pretty nice guy when you got to know him. His gruff exterior was just a façade so the older guys in the club would take him seriously. I appreciated that. I understood it.

We chatted about silly things like what our favorite colors were, what kind of music we liked, and what our favorite movies were. We even talked about our families and our childhoods. Though he mostly knew about mine, I didn't know anything about his and Ice's time with the MC that had kidnapped them. Kiss of Death, it was called. I could see now why he was so protective of Suzie and his brothers. Because it wasn't only Cliff. He was a fierce protector to Gunner and Hannah, Cain and Angel's biological children. It was clear that he had been through a lot in his life even before he came to Bones.

As we rode, he held my hand firmly in his. It felt nice. Comforting as well as proprietary. I liked feeling like I was his. Because he damned sure was mine. Even the thought had me gripping his hand harder. He chuckled and I shot him a look, lifting my chin.

"Hang on as tight as you want, honey. I'm yours. I'm always gonna be yours."

"I have a feeling I'm going to have to stake my claim pretty hard in front of the club girls. You're pretty popular around the clubhouse." Even saying it hurt, but I was going to get past it. My daddy was one of the biggest badasses in the club. And I was his daughter.

"You do what you need to. I've got your back."

"Same as I have yours." I met his gaze with a level one of my own.

As we rode, I noticed that Cyclone was constantly stealing glances at me. I couldn't help but feel a little self-conscious, wondering if I had something on my face or if my hair was a mess. But then I realized that he was just looking at me like I was something special. Like he wanted to admire me from afar and not scare me off with his intensity.

It made my heart swell, and it made me realize just how lucky I was to have him in my life. The start to our relationship may have been unconventional, but it was real, and it was strong and growing stronger with every passing hour. I couldn't help but smile, secure in the knowledge that I was right where I belonged.

We pulled into the compound at two in the afternoon of Christmas Eve. I'd had to stop once to puke, but Cyclone had held my hair back, much like he had in the hotel room. This time, however, when tears streamed from my eyes as I was sick beside the road repeatedly, I not only welcomed his touch, I took comfort in it. Still, I was really glad to be home.

When I got out of the truck, my mother was already running toward me to pull me into her arms.

"I'm so glad you're home. We've got so much to talk about."

I turned to look back toward the clubhouse just in time to see my dad stomp off the porch and straight toward Cyclone.

"Dad!" I called but he didn't look in my direction. Instead, he moved faster and faster to Cyclone.

"Bloody hell…" Cyclone barely got out the words before my dad's fist connected with his face. Once. Then again.

"Dad! Stop!"

I pulled away from my mom, hurrying over to the two hulking men. Cyclone wasn't fighting back, but he was trying to block some of my dad's blows. I think it was more instinctual rather than defensive.

"I said stop!" When I got to the pair, I jumped on my dad's back, shoving my hands over his eyes.

"What the fuck? Willa, get off me!" He backed up several steps, his body tensing as if waiting for a blow.

"Dad, I said stop! Right the fuck now!" I put every ounce of authority I could into my voice, doing my best to sound like I'd heard my dad sound a few times when dressing down a prospect. Or someone who'd brought back a cage empty of gas and full of Red Bull cans. Surprisingly, it worked. *Might* have been that I was still on his back with my hands over his eyes.

"Willa…"

"No. I mean it, Dad. You're not gonna beat up my man just because he knocked me up. Not when he's my choice. No one gets to tell me I can't have him except Cyclone. Not even you or Mom."

"He took advantage of you, sweetheart." When he tugged at my wrist, trying to get my hands off his eyes, I let him. Still didn't climb down in case he got it into his head he was going to go after Cyclone again. "He's probably using you now to hang on to his position in the club. Or his very life. Because I intend to bury that fucker." Yeah. Dad was in Trucker mode. Which wasn't a side he often showed to me or my brother and sisters.

"No, Dad. You're not. You're going to go to Mom

and calm the fuck down. Then we're all gonna sit down and talk about this like civilized fucking adults." I winced. I was in so much trouble once this was over. I'd never spoken to my dad -- or anyone for that matter -- like I had to Dad and Ice. And it had to be two officers in the club. You know. In front of most of the club.

Yeah. Trouble.

"Stand down, Trucker." Ice was leaning against one post on the front porch looking all casual. Like he didn't have a fucking care in the world.

"Big help there, Ice." I gave him a heated look, like I was ready to carve out his liver.

"Hey. Don't look at me. He's a big motherfucker."

"Yes! He is! And I'm five foot nothing and a hundred pounds! And fucking pregnant!" I was losing my patience, my temper redlining. Again.

"Brother, I sure hope this is all pregnancy hormones, 'cause if it ain't, you've got your hands full."

"Watch it, Ice." Dawn, Ice's woman, watched on with amusement, but she gave her man a sidelong glance. "She's gonna be our sister. Do you really want to get on her bad side this early in the game?"

"Point taken, baby."

Cyclone just grinned, even as he spat out a mouthful of blood. "Oh, she read me the Riot Act a couple of times after I got to North Carolina." Cyclone was understandably winded but somehow still on his feet. I'd stopped Trucker from hurting him too much, but my dad could pack quite a punch. "She ain't the shrinking violet everyone always thought she was."

"Of course, I'm not," I snapped, glaring at Cyclone. I couldn't help it. Even in the midst of a beating, he was having fun at my expense. "I'm the daughter of the road captain of Bones MC. I can make up my own fucking mind about who I'm gonna fucking fuck. No one gets to make that decision for me. Not Cyclone. Not Trucker. Me!"

That got everyone's attention. Unfortunately, more than one of the members of Bones were smothering grins. I was about to let loose on some motherfuckers. And where the fuck did that thought come from? I was sweet, Goddamnit!

Thank fuck Shadow's woman, Millie, stepped forward and laid a hand on Trucker's shoulder. "She's right, you know." Her Russian accent was somehow soothing on my frayed nerves. "Have you heard her side of story, Trucker?"

"No." Dad sounded and looked wary as he glanced at me over his shoulder with narrowed eyes. "I haven't. But I heard his side." He pointed to Cyclone. "He admitted she was drunk when he... err... when they... uh..."

"Did the nasty? The hunka chunka? The horizontal tango?"

"Willa..."

"What? You've lived in an MC your entire adult life and you can't say the word 'sex'? Really?"

"Not in relation to my daughter, Willa." He sighed heavily. "Can you please get off me?"

I was still on Dad's back, my legs wrapped around his middle as best I could. He was thick and all muscle, and I wasn't exactly a large or athletic girl. I glanced at Cyclone. Even though he was still breathing hard, he was trying to smother a grin. And failing. So I scowled back at him before answering my dad.

"Depends. You gonna go after my man again?"

"Where's this coming from? Since when are you

interested in boys?"

Mom stepped forward and wrapped her arms around Dad's middle, and I slipped from his back. Millie was there to steady me. The other woman gave me a wink and two thumbs-up before going back to her man. Where Millie's sister, Venus, dressed in hot pink, Millie preferred teal. I was looking forward to the specially made Harley she was having delivered. Should be fun.

"Honey, you know very well she's had a crush on Daniel since before she was a teenager. The fact that she hasn't ever been interested in other boys should clue you in to the fact that man is hers."

"But is she his? Because I still think he's agreeing to make her his old lady just to get out of trouble."

OK, that hurt. I stepped back a couple of steps, my gaze going immediately to Cyclone. Now, instead of amusement at my outburst, he looked like the man I'd always been slightly terrified of. He was the son of the former Bones president. Raised in this life. Trained to be the biggest, baddest warrior he could be. He was also the vice president of the club. Not the man I'd grown to love. Except, they were the same man. Now I was going to see how the two meshed.

"That's enough, Trucker. You can beat on me all you feel like you need to for the way I first claimed your daughter. It's not something I've not beaten myself up over during the six weeks since it happened. But you need to get one thing straight. I do not do anything I don't want to. That includes taking an old lady. No matter how much trouble I'm in. I'll take any punishment I've got coming like a man. I'll even resign as the fucking VP if that's what's demanded. I'll do it all with a smile and a fuckin' princess wave. But I will not make a woman mine unless I'm feeling it here." He pounded his chest. "I'd support her and the baby, if she chose to have it, in any way she saw fit. I'd be part of the kid's life as much as she'd let me. But I would not make her my old lady unless it was something we both wanted."

Cyclone was right up in my dad's face now. My mother still had her arms around Dad, probably to prevent him from lashing out again, and she didn't move.

"Do you love her?" Dad bit out the question between clenched teeth. "I mean, really fuckin' love her?"

I expected Cyclone to tell him what he'd told me. That he was getting there. Instead, without hesitation, he nodded his head crisply. "Abso-fuckin'-lutely I love her. She's smart, beautiful, and so fuckin' fierce she makes me proud. She'll be the best old lady a vice president could ever have, and the best mother to our children. And you can expect there to be more."

"Maybe." I qualified. "Because I'm only six weeks into this little hellion and I'm already sick every fucking day. You want more babies? You better hope and pray this sickness gets better."

That got a laugh from several of the brothers and also seemed to diffuse the situation. Trucker relaxed and allowed Mom to move him away from Cyclone. Cyclone moved to me and pulled me into his arms. He didn't smile or show any of the tenderness he usually reserved for me. Instead, he looked like a warrior ready for an attack. He still tightened his arms around me instead of preparing to defend himself.

"Looks to me like she's made her choice, Trucker. Why not give them a couple of months. See how things go. We can reserve judgment until then."

Trucker pointed a finger at Cyclone. "You better

do right by my daughter, boy. This club killed a motherfucker for her and her mother. Just because you're the VP and one of my best friends' son doesn't mean you won't meet a similar fate if you fuck her over."

"She's my woman, Trucker. I'll protect her with my life and love her until the day I die."

I gasped, burying my face in his chest. Tears were threatening at his declaration. Had been threatening for a few minutes now and I wasn't sure how long I could hold them back.

"See that you do." With that, Mom took Dad back inside the clubhouse. I clung to Cyclone, not wanting to let him go even though I knew I needed to get Mama to look at him.

"Well." Ice grinned down at us. "I guess that settles that. Welcome to the family, sis."

Epilogue

Cyclone

The club Christmas party was in full swing. The old ladies had run off every club girl in the compound and taken over the common room. It currently looked like an explosion of commercialized Christmas. Complete with glitter beards for a few of the guys, a tradition Suzie had started when we'd first come here. I loved every single second of it. Especially since Willa had the most beautiful smile on her face I'd ever seen.

She was wearing a dress I hadn't seen before, and my dick instantly reacted to it as soon as she stepped out of the bathroom. She was stunning.

The emerald gown was made of a soft, luxurious fabric that clung to her curves in all the right places. The neckline was scooped low to show off her cleavage, while the hem stopped mid-thigh and gave a tantalizing glimpse of her smooth legs. With the sleeveless design, her toned arms were shown to perfection. The back dipped low enough to entice any onlooker with its daring design.

Her hair was swept up in a bun with curls and strands spilling freely down her back. The shimmering material reflected the lights of the Christmas tree and there was no way I could keep my eyes -- or my hands -- off her. My fingers itched to get her out of the sexy little number. One thing was for sure, I fully intended to unwrap my present early this Christmas.

I pulled her into my arms and placed a tender kiss on her lips, then stepped back and admired her once again. She was stunning, and I couldn't help but feel like the luckiest bastard in the Goddamned world.

"Merry Christmas, honey," I said, pulling her close for another kiss.

"Merry Christmas, Cyclone." The smile on her face as she looked up at me was brilliant. The chocolate of her eyes sparkled under the lights, and I knew I'd forever remember this moment.

"Come on, you two." Helen came up behind Willa and leaned in to kiss her daughter's cheek. All the women had dressed to the max. All the guys managed to get away with jeans and T-shirts along with our cuts. Helen looked as happy as Willa. Trucker stood behind his wife, scowling at me. I wasn't sure he'd ever be all right with me marrying his daughter, but I was sure he would at least let me live as long as I treated her well. "Cheetah has Willa's property patch and I'm pretty sure Trucker expects you to have a ring, Cyclone." She arched an eyebrow.

"Of course, he does." I snorted.

"And you better not fuckin' disappoint." Trucker scowled at me and it was all I could do not to grin at the big fucker. Yeah, I had a twisted sense of humor.

Instead of responding to him, I pulled a small box from my jeans pocket. The velvet box was light in my hand, and I opened it slowly, revealing a sparkling diamond ring. It wasn't huge or ostentatious. Just a simple marquise cut one-carat stone on a simple gold band. A gasp escaped Willa's lips as she took it in, her eyes wide with surprise.

Her gaze instantly jumped to mine, a look of wonder on her lovely face. "Oh, Cyclone," she breathed, taking the ring from the box and holding it up to the light. "It's beautiful."

"Not as beautiful as you, honey." I took the ring from her and slipped it on the fourth finger of her left hand. It was a perfect fit. Raising her hand to my lips, I dropped a kiss to the back before turning her hand over and kissing her palm. "Not nearly as beautiful as you."

All around us, kids played and laughed. I couldn't help but wonder if our kids would be as happy running around here as I had been as a kid. Those were some of the happiest memories of my life.

My gaze landed on my adopted brother, Gunner, and his twin, Hannah. They were going on sixteen and already finding their place within the club. In some ways, I thought Hannah was even more of a force to be reckoned with than Gunner. I grinned, hoping if we had a girl she'd be just like my sister.

Adults ate and drank. A couple of the kids' dogs bounded around the room looking for scraps and cuddles. But the only person I saw was Willa. Well, until Trucker stepped up beside me.

"I still owe you a beatin', you bastard." Yeah. Gonna be a long road with this one.

"Dad, you promised." Willa frowned at her father. She'd opted to take the hard line with him, not backing down an inch. She'd claimed me in front of most of all the officers and most of the club, and she stood by that claim. A couple of the club girls had given her pushback, but at least one of those girls now avoided Willa like the plague. I had no idea what went down and apparently only Willa and Dawn were around when it happened, but I was proud of my woman for standing her ground. She'd lived in the club all her life and knew what she had to do to defend her territory. It was good to know she could and would. I was one lucky bastard.

"I got eyes on you, Cyclone. I will be watching. You mistreat my daughter, me and you gonna have a round."

I grinned. "No worries there." I smiled down at my woman. "Willa has my heart."

Trucker just grunted, still looking disgruntled.

As the night went on, the party began to wind down. Most of the club members and their women and children dispersed, and only a few stragglers remained. Willa and I stood in the center of the room, lost in our own world. A couple of the brothers gave me shit about being pussy whipped, but I just flipped them off. Several of them had their own women they adored so I knew there was no real heat in their ribbing.

I brushed a strand of hair out of her face and tucked it behind her ear. "I'm sorry we got off on the wrong foot after we both sobered up, Willa. I handled myself badly."

She grinned up at me. "Yes. You did. But you came through in the end, so I forgive you."

I smiled back, relieved. "You're an incredible woman, you know that?"

Willa chuckled. "I am indeed."

We were silent for a few moments, lost in our own thoughts. Then, she spoke softly. "I love you, Cyclone. I think I always have."

"I love you too, honey." I winked at her. "Let's get out of here. I need to unwrap my present."

"Oh?" Her arms slid around my neck, and she pressed her body against mine.

"Yeah. It's currently wrapped in a shimmering green gown. Got me hard as fuck."

Her grin turned positively wicked. "In that case, let's get going."

We left the common room and made our way to our rooms inside the Bones clubhouse on the third floor with the other officers' quarters. As I shut the door and pulled Willa into my arms, I couldn't help but feel like the luckiest man in the Goddamned world.

I had a club of brothers who'd lay down their lives for me, the woman I loved by my side, and my child growing in her belly.

I had the best Christmas I'd ever imagined. I had my woman. And I was never letting her go.

Marteeka Karland

International bestselling author Marteeka Karland leads a double life as an action romance writer by evening and a semi-domesticated housewife by day. Known for her down-and-dirty MC romances, Marteeka takes pleasure in spinning tales of tenacious, protective heroes and spirited heroines. She staunchly advocates that every character deserves a blissful ending.

Marteeka finds joy in baking and gardening with her husband. Make sure to visit her website to stay updated with her most recent projects. Don't forget to register for her newsletter which will pepper you with a potpourri of Teeka's beloved recipes, book suggestions, autograph events, and a plethora of interesting tidbits.

Marteeka at Changeling: changelingpress.com/marteeka-karland-a-39

Want more? Wanda Violet O. is Teeka's Dark Erotica side.

Bones MC Multiverse

Contemporary MC and Crossovers

Bones MC
Shadow Demons
Salvation's Bane MC
Black Reign MC
Iron Tzars MC
Grim Road MC
Bones MC Legends
Kiss of Death MC

Print and Audio

Bones MC Audio
Salvation's Bane MC Audio
Iron Tzars MC Audio
Bones MC Print Duets
Grim Road MC Audio

Changeling Press LLC

Contemporary Action Adventure, Sci-Fi, Steampunk, Dark Fantasy, Urban Fantasy, Paranormal, and BDSM Romance available in e-book, audio, and print format at ChangelingPress.com – MC Romance, Werewolves, Vampires, Dragons, Shapeshifters and Horror -- Tales from the edge of your imagination.

Where can I get Changeling Press Books?

Changeling Press e-books are available at ChangelingPress.com, Amazon, Apple Books, Barnes & Noble, Kobo, Smashwords, and other online retailers, including Everand Subscription and Kobo Subscription Services. Print books are available at Amazon, Barnes and Noble, and by ISBN special order through your local bookstores.

Changeling Press, LLC

ChangelingPress.com

www.ingramcontent.com/pod-product-compliance
Lightning Source LLC
Chambersburg PA
CBHW060551260626
47161CB00003B/1143